"I Guess It's True—You Never Forget The First Time,"

David said.

Amanda closed her eyes and kept them shut. "David, please don't dredge all that up."

"I'm not dredging—you can't pretend it didn't happen. It's part of you and part of me. The first time we made love was right here, and that's not so terrible." He pivoted and faced her, his blue eyes warm, his voice suddenly kind.

She shook her head. "It was one long mistake. We were so far from perfect for each other. Why on earth did we ever do it?"

David looked at her mouth, her chin and then back to her exposed throat. He watched her blouse as it rose and fell with her erratic breathing. "Because touching you was all I knew of heaven," he whispered.

Dear Reader,

November is a time for giving thanks, and this year I have an awful lot to be thankful for—my family, my friends and my terrific job. Because it's through my job that I get to bring to you, the readers, books written by fabulous authors. These are love stories that will give you a lift when you're down, that will make you laugh and cry and rediscover the unique joy of falling in love.

This November has so *many* wonderful stories, starting with the latest in Annette Broadrick's SONS OF TEXAS series, *Marriage Texas Style!* (If you missed the earlier SONS OF TEXAS, don't worry, because this volume also stands alone.)

Next, there's our *Man of the Month* ex-sky jockey Kyle Gordon. Kyle is cocky, opinionated, sexy—altogether he's perfect, and he more than meets his match in schoolteacher Susan Brooks.

November is completed with Barbara Boswell's *Double Trouble* (don't ask me to explain the plot—just read the book), Joan Johnston's *Honey and the Hired Hand,* Doreen Owens Malek's *Arrow in the Snow* (welcome back, Doreen!), and Leslie Davis Guccione's *A Rock and a Hard Place.*

So take time from your busy holiday schedule to curl up with a good Desire book. I know I'm going to!

All the best,

Lucia Macro
Senior Editor

LESLIE DAVIS GUCCIONE

A ROCK AND A HARD PLACE

SILHOUETTE *Desire*®

Published by Silhouette Books New York

America's Publisher of Contemporary Romance

SILHOUETTE BOOKS
300 East 42nd St., New York, N.Y. 10017

A ROCK AND A HARD PLACE

ISBN: 0-373-05748-2

First Silhouette Books printing November 1992

Printed in the U.S.A.

Books by Leslie Davis Guccione

Silhouette Desire

Before the Wind #279
*Bittersweet Harvest #311
*Still Waters #353
*Something in Common #376
*Branigan's Touch #523
*Private Practice #554
A Gallant Gentleman #674
Rough and Ready #713
A Rock and a Hard Place #748

*Branigan Brothers series

LESLIE DAVIS GUCCIONE

lives with her husband and three children in a state of semichaos in an historic sea captains' district south of Boston. When she's not at her typewriter, she's actively researching everything from sailboats to cranberry bogs. What free time she has is spent sailing and restoring her circa 1827 Cape Cod cottage. Her ideas for her books are based on the world around her—as she states, "Romance is right under your nose." She has also written under the name Leslie Davis.

To Isabel Swift and Gail Chasan—
I finally got it right!

One

Simply put, his entrance into the room stopped the presentation cold. It was the stuff B-movies are made of. Amanda Mendenhall's heart leaped into free-fall, dragging her train of thought with it. She stared at him; he stared right back. The men seated around the boardroom table stared at them both.

At the head of the table Amanda was caught in midsentence, hand raised in explanation. "Mendenhall and Lipton's experience in public relations..."

Four of the men responsible for the Oakhurst account, the restoration of a historic mill site on the Brandywine River, turned as the fifth came through the doorway.

"Excuse me, gentlemen. Unavoidable delay." The architect breezed in, the apology on his lips. "Please—" He, too, let the remainder of his sentence drift as he caught sight of her.

Matthew Oakhurst stood up. "Come right in, David. This is Amanda Mendenhall of Mendenhall and Lipton. Miss Mendenhall, David Smith, chief architect for the mill restoration."

Amanda extended her hand and willed it not to tremble. "Mr. Smith."

He registered only the faintest surprise. "Miss Mendenhall. Please continue.... I hope Matt told you I'd be late."

She nodded. Matthew Oakhurst had said *the architect* would be late. He'd never mentioned who the architect was.

David Smith's chestnut hair, as thick and unruly as ever, looked as though he'd rushed through the September afternoon to get there. His handsome face was flushed, but it was impossible to tell whether his high color was from his professional hours outdoors or the shock they'd both received.

Amanda willed her mind to return to the business at hand, and as soon as David sat down, she continued her explanations, passed around examples of her agency's work and pulled out the stops on her one-woman presentation.

"Gentlemen, Mendenhall and Lipton has the capabilities this project requires. To emphasize the significance of the historic site, we'll deliver advertising from print media to radio and television spots, as well as a complete public-relations campaign. We're a full-service agency, prepared to take the account from concept and keep it in the public eye right through to completion. We'll market not only here in the Brandywine Valley, but wherever applicable along the Mid-Atlantic corridor."

She paused long enough to make eye contact with each of the men and then forced a smile into a wide, self-confident grin.

Leo Brachman, contractor for the project, arched his eyebrows and glanced at brother Ira. Matthew Oakhurst, founder of Oakhurst Design Group, nodded. John Wilkins of the Conservation Council smiled politely. Not one of the men was under fifty-five—except David, who was thirty-one, exactly four months older than she.

Amanda watched David take his reading glasses from his jacket. She remembered wire frames. These were horn-rimmed. He'll pat his empty pocket, she thought. He did, and she flushed.

She made eye contact with John Wilkins as if that would keep her glance from wandering. "The mill site means a great deal to me, gentlemen. I spent my childhood studying those ruins, playing along the ledge over the Brandywine River. Many a friend home with me for a school holiday was treated to a picnic there. The property has a very special significance." The corners of David's mouth twitched.

Amanda's memorized conclusion blurred. "I'm well acquainted with the mill's history, its physical layout and the potential of this undertaking. My agency would like a chance to show you what we could do for the Brandywine Mill Project. I promise you won't be disappointed."

This time her smile was a trifle less spontaneous, but riveting, nevertheless. Leo and Ira smiled back. John nodded at Matthew. David Smith, reading her work samples, missed it.

"I for one would like to see what your group can do," Matthew replied. "And I'm sure David agrees with me."

Silence draped the room as the men deferred to the younger architect. Still on her feet, at the head of the table, Amanda waited.

David pulled his glasses off and set them on the brochure in front of him. "By all means. Let's see what she can do for us."

Amanda's reply was terse. "I take that as a vote of confidence, Mr. Smith. You won't be sorry."

David looked at her. "Do you have a copy of the blueprints?"

"No."

"You'll need them. I'll get them to you. Better still, stop by our office. Come and take a look at the scale model. A photograph of it might make a good brochure cover. Of course, that's your area of expertise, not mine."

"Thank you," she replied as she collected the samples being passed back across the gleaming mahogany table. When her well-worn portfolio was zipped, she opened her calendar. "Shall we agree on a date for my presentation?"

"Three weeks? Ground breaking is scheduled for the end of October. I'm sure you'll want to be there for publicity purposes if you get the account. The sooner we choose an agency the better, but we'll need time to consider all the competition. Am I being unreasonable?" David's smile rivaled hers for sparkle.

No more than you ever were, she thought.

They settled on the last week of the month, and within fifteen minutes business was concluded. Amanda thanked each of the men sincerely for the opportunity to bid on the account. She shook hands first with David. By the time she'd come around to Leo Brachman, the sensation of David's touch no longer lingered on her fingers.

She excused herself and left the contractors, architects and Conservation Council representative talking among themselves. The tension headache she always got after these sessions was threatening, and she wanted only to get back to her office for the aspirin and tea that were her panacea. Once in the privacy of her office, she'd try to make sense of what had just happened.

David Smith put his glasses back into his pocket as his associates discussed the presentation. He managed an appropriate response, then offered the excuse of an on-site problem and fled. His defenses were up, but adrenaline still surged through him as he searched for Amanda among the bustle on Eleventh Street. He caught sight of her at a stoplight. September in Wilmington, Delaware, was warm and breezy, and for a fraction of a moment he drank in the impression she made as she faced the wind and swept back her chin-length hair, lighter than his by a shade or two.

She had a good, expensive cut, set off by understated but well-made clothes. No different than before, but a darn sight easier for her now, he thought as he watched her step off the curb.

Before. How long had it been since he'd thought about her? How long since the sight of her made his breath catch in his chest? "Remarkable," David whispered with an unconscious sigh. He started after her at a brisk pace and reached hailing distance at the edge of Rodney Square. "Amanda."

She kept walking.

"Amanda, for heaven's sake."

He approached on her left. In easy strides he passed her, swung into her path and stood stock-still on the sidewalk. "Amanda, you owe me an explanation. At least tell me what you're doing in Wilmington."

Although he topped six feet, the hilly incline of Eleventh Street was steep and put him eye to eye with her five feet nine inches. There were smudges on the knees of his khaki trousers and a beeper peeked from his belt as he pushed back his sport jacket to jam his hands into his pockets. He was without a tie. He rocked back on his heels and looked into her coffee-colored eyes. His own were wide with frank curiosity. The breeze played in his hair.

"David, please."

"Please what?" He watched as she glanced down at her leather portfolio.

She started past him, then marched forward onto King Street.

He matched her stride and continued in the direction of the river. "A woman I haven't seen in six years suddenly shows up to bid on publicizing my project, and I'm supposed to let her walk back out into the sunset? When you left New York, I thought you took all that talent to Washington State."

"I'm back from Seattle." She quickened her steps and rounded the corner, passing a bar and a sidewalk café.

He looked at his watch. "So it seems. It's nearly three o'clock. Let me buy you a drink, and you can bring me up to date."

"David, please."

"David, please...David, please. Dazzle, you can do better than that after six years."

Amanda stopped walking, well past the bar, and looked at him. "I don't want to do better than that. One of the things I liked least about you was your perverse sense of humor. When *you* left New York, I thought you took all that talent to your own firm in Philadelphia."

"I did."

"The time for buying me a drink and bringing me up to date would have been well *before* my presentation to the Oakhurst Group. I don't think it's a bit funny that you let me waltz in there without so much as a phone call to let me know this was your design. Do you have any idea what the Oakhurst account means to me?"

She nodded in answer to her own question. "Of course you do. I bet you've been laughing yourself silly at your drawing board as you plotted this. You know as well as I do what happened at that mill. During the entire presentation, I was terrified you would make some snide reference to it. You ruined my concentration."

She was more defensive than he remembered, but every bit as feisty. David had the audacity to grin. "That old place still holds memories after all these years?"

"Tease all you want. You know exactly what I'm referring to."

"But you can't bring yourself to say it." He chuckled, challenged by the fire in her eyes. "Some things never change. My sense of humor may be the same, but so is your conclusion jumping. Dazzle, time heals all wounds. Six years is a long time."

"Stop calling me Dazzle," she muttered as she began to cross the street.

"I'd forgotten how it suits you. Even now you still have that dazzling look. You sparkled in that office just now."

"No thanks to you."

"Your accusation that I set you up is ridiculous."

"Why? It's a lot more logical for me to be in this town than you. Wilmington, Delaware, is the last place on earth I'd expect to find you, let alone working for someone else."

"Things change." David's beeper sounded and he touched his waist. "So much for small talk. I need to get to a phone. Come with me."

"David, please."

"There you go again." He looked back at the café. "I have to answer my page and call the office. If you won't talk about last time, we at least need to straighten out *this time*." David watched her wince. "Ah, the tension headaches. Aspirin and tea still do the trick? We could get some right over there."

"No, thank you."

"Suit yourself. You always did." He dropped to one knee and grasped her portfolio.

"David, get up!" she hissed as she tugged it.

"I just wanted to see if you ground off the monogram." He turned her leather case in his hands. "AMS. Son of a gun, you didn't." From his knees he watched half a dozen emotions cross her face before she lifted the portfolio defensively to her breasts.

"I have hours of work ahead of me," she murmured.

David stood and watched as she set off toward Stowman Place. He let her go, aware that his heart had maintained its erratic thumping through the entire episode.

Two

In another minute Amanda had walked down Stowman Place to the now-fashionable brick row house, home to Mendenhall and Lipton. She looked through the cityscape in the direction of the park where the serpentine Brandywine opened into the Delaware. "Stupid river," she muttered. "Damn stupid river. Stupid project."

She entered her office still muttering. At the desk she handed over the contents of her portfolio to Karen Winters, office manager-cum-receptionist, with a curt "File these, will you?"

Karen pulled the samples out. "Under *Brachman, Oakhurst, Brandywine* or *Not a Chance?*"

"Do I look that discouraged?"

"You're not dancing on air."

"I should be. They're giving us a shot at the account. I have to make the final presentation at the end of the month."

Karen whistled.

"Hold my calls. I have a lot of thinking to do," Amanda replied as she read one of the message slips. "When did Toys Galore call?"

"Half an hour ago."

Amanda looked at the closed door to her right. "Marco's in?"

Karen nodded. "He hasn't stopped creating masterpieces since you left. He told me to tell you that. Pop a few aspirin, I'll brew some tea." She swiveled to answer the jangling phone. "Mendenhall and Lipton, may I help you?"

Amanda took her headache medication, then knocked once and entered her art director's office. She fanned the air in front of her nose in an attempt to lighten the smell of rubber cement and permanent markers. "Get some ventilation in here, or I'll be scraping you off the ceiling."

Her disheveled associate looked up from his drawing board. Two markers and a ruler stuck out of the chest pocket of his Hawaiian shirt, and for reasons known only to himself a bandanna dangled from a safety pin where the hip pocket of his well-worn jeans used to be. "If it doesn't reek of solvent and glue in here, how'll you know I've been working?"

"Because I won't be getting phone messages from clients asking where on earth their pasteups are. Toys Galore—"

"Small potatoes."

"Don't insult the client. A hard-won collection of small potatoes pays your salary." Amanda slumped as she sat on the stool, the only uncluttered spot in a room jammed with illustration boards, typeface books and innumerable other items connected with commercial art, including a calendar of scantily clad women on which Karen had scrawled Sexist Swine.

Her twenty-eight-year-old creative associate pointed at the drawing board. "Nearly done, boss. There's nothing like sinking your teeth into a full-page spread of bicycles and dolls to make you feel productive."

Amanda looked at his work, found an error and reversed the copy under the clip art of two bikes. "How can I promote you when you can't tell the difference between a dirt bike and a ten-speed?"

Marco sighed, genuinely apologetic. "I would have caught it in the proof."

"The client would have caught it in your pasteup. Do I need to look at the rest of it?"

"A second pair of eyes, less tired than mine, wouldn't hurt," he replied seriously. "I'm flat-out, Amanda."

"It's only going to get worse."

Marco looked at her thoughtfully, then laughed. "Hot damn, they liked you! I knew you could melt the Brachmans. Hello, Brandywine Mill Project."

"Slow down. All I got was a chance to make a presentation and bid on the account. There's no guarantee."

"Guarantee? If I wanted guarantees, I'd have a union job like my old man. We can strut our stuff with this one, Amanda."

"Enough clichés. Finish your small potato. I'll proof it with you in twenty minutes, and Karen can run it over to Toys Galore on her way home."

"Seriously, the mill restoration is our big chance."

"Seriously, you're right, and we've got to put heart and soul into it." She left the room as Marco uttered one of his usual obscenities and turned back to his rubber cement.

At five-twenty, with Karen and the Toys Galore pasteup gone to the client, Amanda sat at her desk. She raised her head as Marco entered. Without asking he came around behind her and massaged her shoulders while looking at the room. "This office is too upwardly mobile, boss. You need to loosen it up, just like these neck muscles."

She relaxed as he worked. "We've had this conversation before. I like my taste."

Behind her he chuckled. "What does this room say about you? A diploma from the University of Pennsylvania, a framed hunting print, a leather chair... tasteful, conservative, boring. How about a calendar of naked men and some Georgia O'Keeffe posters? Her work has a nice hint of eroticism. I could paint a mural over the filing cabinets."

Amanda laughed at the familiar jibes and rotated her neck as his thumbs worked at her hairline. "I shudder to think what you'd put in a mural. Stop worrying about me and knock off the insinuations about my private life."

"Or your lack of one."

"Marco."

"What's a business associate for?"

"For business. And while we're on that subject, you can begin work on the Oakhurst account by picking up a set of blueprints from the Oakhurst Design Group office on your way in tomorrow."

"Me, the semibearded, eccentric advertising genius you keep hidden away in the office?"

"Can I trust you to shave and shake hands?"

"No spiked hair and rhinestone stud in my ear?"

As exhausted as she was, Amanda appreciated the humor. She put one of her hands over each of Marco's as he continued to massage her taut shoulders.

By the time David Smith entered the foyer of Mendenhall and Lipton, the receptionist's desk was empty. He followed the sound of voices to the open office doorway ahead of him, then cleared his throat as Amanda patted the hands of whoever was massaging her shoulders.

"Am I disturbing anything?"

"I'd like to think so," the fellow replied as Amanda pushed his hands off her collarbone and shot into ramrod-straight posture.

"David!"

As she made a pretense of dusting herself off, David extended his hand. "David Smith. I'm the Oakhurst architect for the mill project. Amanda needs these blueprints. I thought I'd drop them off, since I know how anxious the agency is to get started. Would you be Lipton?"

The fellow took the renderings and chuckled. "Lipton, as in Mendenhall and? No. Marco D'Abruzzi, art director."

David looked at Amanda. "Is there a Lipton?"

"Absolutely," Marco replied.

Amanda glared at both of them. "Thank you, David. I'm sure this was out of your way."

He waved off the statement. "I had an urge to see your operation. After all these years—"

"Thank you for the blueprints. Maybe another time when we're not so busy." She rose from her chair and came around the desk.

Marco arched his eyebrows. "David Smith. Familiar name."

"Common enough," David answered.

"Half a dozen in any phone book," Amanda threw in.

"Architect? About thirty-one, possibly from Pittsburgh?"

"Marco was just leaving. See you in the morning," Amanda added.

"She's trying to get rid of me—a dead giveaway," the art director continued as he glanced at the monogram of the portfolio lying on the desk. "Smith, as in the University of Pennsylvania, maybe graduate work at Princeton and some lean years in the Big Apple?"

David glanced at Amanda. "All's not forgotten."

She seemed to have found her voice, and there was murder in it. "Marco, put a lid on it. Thank you for the blueprints, David. This wasn't necessary, though. My art director was to pick them up in the morning."

David stared right into her deep-as-ever eyes. "May I assume from your disposition that your partner Lipton will be handling our account rather than you?"

"No."

"Is Lipton male or female?"

"Male. Used to be, anyway, poor fellow," Marco replied.

Amanda turned. "May I remind you, D'Abruzzi, that David Smith, no matter who else you think he might be, represents the Oakhurst account?"

"Lipton was your idea, not mine. Hasn't the architect got a sense of humor?"

"Quite a few people think so," David replied. The repartee amused him, and the fact that Amanda was so obviously fighting for composure continued to buoy his spirits.

Amanda took a deep breath. "All right. Lipton is my neutered cat."

David laughed. "A sense of humor after all these years. Clever name, clever name."

"A stroke of creative genius for an ad agency," Marco added.

"I meant for a cat," David added. "No doubt it has something to do with your fondness for tea."

"A memory like a steel trap," Marco whispered.

Amanda picked up her linen jacket, her purse and the blueprints. "Gentlemen, it's been a very long day."

"That means she wants to lock up," Marco said as he crossed the reception area. "Sneaky, though. She's apt to wolf down something greasy and disgusting and then come back."

"Conscientious," David replied. "Always was."

"A regular workaholic. Makes my fourteen-hour days look pitiful," Marco called as he grabbed his things from his own office and came back to them.

David put his hands in his pockets and turned to Amanda. "I remember. Any chance I can meet you back here about seven, Dazzle? We have a few things to set straight."

"Of course not."

"Dazzle?" Marco repeated.

David put his palms up. "A slip of the tongue."

"No doubt earned back in those undergraduate days," Marco said.

"Never mind! Out!"

David followed Marco out onto the sidewalk.

"I'm going home to my cat, a hot bath and a dinner date," Amanda added as she locked the door.

There had been an episode in a hot bath. Candles, David recalled, and bubbles. Had it been a birthday? They'd been celebrating something he no longer remembered. "Amanda, we need to clear up some things. It's important. We can discuss it privately, or if you insist, here with Marco."

"Please insist here with Marco," the art director added. "A whole new Amanda Mendenhall is unfolding right before my eyes."

Amanda spoke directly to David. "No, it isn't important. At the moment there are more pressing things on my agenda. If you'll both excuse me, I'm late already."

The dramatic exit might have worked if she'd left the men on the sidewalk, but it appeared that they all were parked in the private lot behind the building. David grinned as Amanda stomped down the alley with a man on either side of her.

Marco unlocked his car and called out, "Nice to have met you, Smith," as he started the engine.

David waved to him and turned to Amanda as she unlocked the door to a sleek sports model. "This suits you. I pictured you in something like this. Somehow public city transit systems seemed temporary."

"I earned this myself. What I drive shouldn't concern you. Nothing but the job I intend to do for the mill restoration should concern you. Excuse me. I have someone waiting."

He put his arm on the door. "Amanda, we've hurt each other enough for a lifetime. I won't let you get into the car thinking I'd dream up anything as stupid or immature as surprising you in the midst of an agency presentation. I've tried to forget a lot these past six years, but I do remember what your work means to you."

"But you must have known. The name—"

"The old, established, moneyed Mendenhalls fill a Delaware phone book. The Amanda I knew wanted to get away from it. Seattle's proof of that. I've been in business for myself for three years, then I joined Oakhurst last fall—their Philadelphia office. Until today I hadn't so much as set foot in Wilmington. I haven't paid attention to the ad agencies bidding on our mill project. When Matt told me Mendenhall and Lipton was presenting this afternoon, I thought it might be some cousin or other of yours. I even gave some thought to asking about you. Damn it, you were on the West Coast, last I heard." He watched her as he talked, stirred by her wariness and the flicker of doubt in her eyes.

"Truly?"

"Cross my heart."

"Then I apologize."

"That's it, after all that malicious accusal?"

She was trying not to smile. "Why is everything funny, David?"

"Your self-righteous indignation always was. All that fury and temper have got you glowing. You're as irritating as ever and just as beautiful. Have you changed at all?"

She got into the car and he looked down at her, holding the glance long enough to catch a hint of something far more unsettling than wariness. Amanda sighed. "No. I'm still the irritating, self-righteous person you remember."

"That's not what I meant."

"Well, it's the best I can do."

"You must admit, this afternoon has been one for the books. Loosen up. It was all coincidence. You made a mistake."

"All right, I made a mistake. Under the circumstances you can hardly blame me."

"For once let's keep blame out of this." His head swam with questions. He could feel his caution slipping. "How long have you been back?"

"About a year."

"I assume you have no plans for returning to Seattle?"

"No, I'm home to stay."

"Did you leave a string of broken hearts out there, too? Did you mend your own?"

"You see! It doesn't pay to give you an inch."

"I'll take a mile? This is more than idle curiosity. I assume the Oakhurst account is one you'll hang your hat on. The restoration of that flour mill from derelict Revolutionary War site to historic landmark and educational center would be the brass ring on your carousel."

"That's one way to put it. The Oakhurst Design Group is the best in the area. If you've joined them permanently, then this part of the country will just have to hold both of us."

"I'm not sure you think that's possible, Amanda. What if you win the account?"

"No *ifs*. I will win the account, and I'll do a terrific job. I've worked long and hard to start my own agency and I've got a very good professional reputation, one that includes Marco. He's a fabulous art director."

"But what you really want to add is that Menden-halls have tilled this soil since the Vikings arrived. It's your turf, not mine."

"Your words, not mine."

"Resentment?"

"Some."

"After all this time, I'm surprised you have that much feeling left for me, even animosity."

"Don't flatter yourself. It's the circumstances I hate."

"Out of principle?"

"Principle and ethics. While I'm working on the account I have to have as little to do with you as possible."

"And afterward?"

She looked surprised. "When my business with Oakhurst is complete, we'll go our separate ways." She started her car.

"I'll hold you to that, Dazzle."

Although she stayed silent, she blushed, and David pressed his fist to his breastbone, against the threat of unwelcome heat. For too long there had been nothing there but regret and anger, emotions he'd carried in his chest as hot and heavy as molten lead. He cleared his throat as he willed the pain to dissipate. "We're stuck together temporarily. Look at it this way—there's no-where to go but up. We have to do better as business associates than we ever did as husband and wife."

Three

———

Stowman Place, even in morning traffic, was only a ten-minute drive from Amanda's house farther up the river in one of the city's older neighborhoods on the edge of Brandywine Park. Normally she used the commute to listen to the radio and review commercials she'd placed in drive time on local stations.

Nothing, however, about the beginning of September was normal, and for the moment all she hoped to accomplish was to make sense of what was happening. The smell of coffee and the muffled strains of rock music from Marco's office greeted her as she entered her building at eight-thirty the next morning.

Her own office was as she'd left it, with the exception of a strip of professionally lettered illustration board the size of a business envelope. Dazzle & D'Abruzzi, Advertising Specialists sat propped on her blotter. She picked it up.

"D'Abruzzi!"

He was already in the doorframe. "I thought you'd like it. Packs a punch, don't you think?"

"You know I don't like it. You know I hate it."

"Which part do you hate, Dazzle or D'Abruzzi?"

"I know you're joking but, Marco, this is a very bad day for jokes."

"Jokes? I'm not the one who dreamed up a fictitious business partner named after a cat, which was named after a tea bag."

"It was an impetuous decision. I needed something to differentiate us from the Mendenhall law firm and the Mendenhall brokerage house."

"While still cashing in on the family name. That's what I told David this morning."

Amanda put the illustration board down. "Run that past me again," she replied, taking a step closer to him. "You shaved." He was also in pleated navy pants, a pin-striped shirt and conservative necktie.

Marco bowed. "The full nine yards. Oakhurst Design Group didn't seem the rhinestone-earring type. I had breakfast with their junior partner this morning. Talked business mostly. Quite a sense of humor, your ex-husband has. He didn't remember that you had much of one, though. This cat thing really made him howl. Excuse the pun."

Amanda grabbed a fistful of his necktie and pulled him a step closer. "You've had breakfast with David at the Oakhurst office?"

Both she and Marco ignored the ringing at the receptionist's desk. It stopped abruptly after the third ring.

Marco loosened her grip and smoothed the tie against his chest. "Watch the silk, boss. You don't pay me enough to replace it."

"In about two seconds you'll be on unemployment."

Marco patted her shoulder. "Amanda, you don't want to have anything to do with him. One of us has to carry the account. I'm going out to the mill site this morning to shoot some glossies, take a look around. That's all I was arranging."

"Excuse me, Marco, phone's for you." Amanda jumped as David Smith's voice, deep and startling, brought her around. Again he filled the doorframe, looking self-satisfied and amused. "Forgive me for answering it. You two were deep in discussion and there's nobody out there at the desk." There was a pause as David turned to Amanda. "I did tell Marco I'd pick him up at eight forty-five. No sense in taking two cars."

"I'll go," Amanda blurted, ignoring the perusal she got. Heaven only knew what had already been discussed between them. "Marco, go take your phone call and get back to work. We do have other deadlines."

"Whatever you say," Marco replied as he loosened the knot of his tie and returned to his office.

David leaned against the doorjamb and looked her over. "Short skirt, silk blouse. You're not dressed for rock climbing."

"I'll manage. My shoes have flat heels."

"Leather soles. No slipping on ledges or picking your way through the mire. I'm on a tight schedule."

"So am I."

Karen arrived as they began to leave. "My goodness," she murmured, her eyes wide.

"Introduce yourself. Professional credentials only," Amanda muttered to David as she stepped into her art director's office for the camera. She turned away and wagged her finger at Marco. "Not one word to Karen about any of this, no games, no teasing. She doesn't know a thing about David, and it's to stay that way."

"Your diploma reads Amanda Mendenhall Smith and your portfolio monogram's AMS. She's never asked?"

"There are millions of Smiths in this world."

"And he's stumbled back into yours." Marco put his hand over his heart. "Okay, okay. On my mother's lasagna, no monkey business. Can I trust the two of you out there at the mill?"

She put her hands on his drawing board. "Do you have any idea how many job applications I get from art directors?"

Marco looked past her and through the door. "It's not me you need to worry about."

Amanda went back to the architect, who was sitting on the edge of the receptionist's desk, deep in a discussion about Wilmington's changing skyline. Karen looked like butter left too close to the stove.

"Shall we go?"

Once outside, David chuckled as they got into his four-wheel-drive automobile. "The rest of Mendenhall seemed to like me well enough. That leaves only your cat. What Lipton thinks remains to be seen."

"Charm was always one of your strong suits." Amanda leaned back as they maneuvered through city traffic and headed north toward the state line. "I don't want you socializing with my staff."

"It's a little early in the day to be so feisty."

"I don't want to get back into a verbal jousting match with you. I'm sure you've gotten the impression that our...past relationship...is an open book. It's not. Karen Winters has no idea who you are. Marco's the only one. I asked him just now to keep it to himself."

"And you can trust him? As much as you trust any man, that is?"

Amanda turned her head, but David kept his eyes, still disconcertingly blue, on Pennsylvania Avenue.

"Marco's got a wild personality, but he's enormously talented and, yes, I trust him. There is a serious side to him. He's the creative backbone of the agency."

"He said the same thing about you."

"Did he? We work well together."

"Is he in love with you?"

They pulled away from an intersection, and Amanda looked out the window at the grand houses lining the wide boulevard. "No."

"I get the impression he was, once."

Amanda chose her words carefully. "David, this whole bizarre situation is extremely uncomfortable for me. I was up all night trying to make sense of it, trying not to let what we were—"

"You and Marco?"

"You and me, David. I don't want what's happened before to get in the way of my job."

"We were lovers. We were married, Amanda. After six years are you still choking on the words?"

"That's what I mean. All this dredging has me worried sick. You're too damn good-looking for your own good. Karen's already flirting her heart out."

"My looks are the problem? And all the time I thought it was my position with Oakhurst that has you unglued."

"I am not unglued."

"Sorry. Your receptionist's behavior was flattering. She's fun."

"She's my employee and so is Marco. You two men are cut from the same cloth. You've got the same perverse sense of humor."

"And taste in women."

"Stop that! I want your word that you'll refrain from any kind of socializing. Not talking about me. No telling stories about us. No dates with Karen. No hanging out with Marco."

David looked at her briefly. Amanda damned her memory, memory that continued to flood her brain at the least provocation. Everything about him was familiar. Every stare spoke volumes. She had neither the time nor the temperament to contemplate the gnawing need racing through her to make David Smith aware, acutely aware, that she was capable, successful and happy without him.

"You're serious," he was saying.

"Never more so. Does Matthew Oakhurst know?"

"Know what?"

"You know very well what."

"Say it, Amanda."

The lush, moneyed suburbs north of Wilmington slid past the window. Her hesitancy left her wide open for teasing, and she knew it. "Does Matthew Oakhurst know we were married?" she asked finally.

"Are you afraid of my answer? Afraid that the minute you left the room yesterday I gathered up Matt, the Brachmans, even Wilkins from the Conservation

Council and told them? Do you think I told them the no-nonsense businesswoman who'd just made her presentation had spent five years in a string of apartments surviving on peanut butter and jelly with me, back in another life?''

"I should have known you'd joke."

"The account's your brass ring. Give me a little credit for discretion."

"Can I?" Amanda replied.

"I don't suppose it's occurred to you that I have no desire for them to know that I was married to you, either.''

Amanda blushed. Humiliation heated her scalp and cheeks, but she didn't apologize. There had already been a lifetime of apologies.

David swung the car off the main road and into Montchanin, increasingly spare countryside still dotted with multimillion-dollar hilltop estates. There was a time when Amanda would have expected him to comment on the architecture, but neither of them was watching the scenery.

"Amanda, everything isn't a joke with me. How hard I've worked, how far I've come, what I've earned is no joke. There have been other failures I've overcome. I separate my social life from my professional, too. Discussing you is not something I do casually, ever."

"Then we see eye to eye." Before she lost her emotional footing she turned to him. "This project includes federal funds, minority hiring requirements, nonprofit foundation grants. If anyone thought for a minute that you and I had some connection, the situation could be completely misconstrued."

"We couldn't have that."

"No, we couldn't. It was tough enough convincing the Brachmans and your boss to listen to me. For advertising and public relations they want someone who can quote football statistics, someone born during the Eisenhower administration. It's infuriating that the fact that I don't happen to have male apparatus or twenty years of experience should have any bearing on this. I don't want anything more to jeopardize M and L's chances, David. All I'm asking is that you leave well enough alone. Don't say anything about a foolish mistake we both made a long time ago."

"This is the definitive account, the one you and Marco make your reputations on."

"I hope he told you that this morning."

"He did, Amanda, and he was serious. He was serious about a lot of things."

They reached the Delaware-Pennsylvania line. The stately homes built from financial and chemical empires stood farther apart on their green lawns and down their private driveways. David nodded at a pair of fieldstone gateposts. "Your Aunt Dora's, if I'm not mistaken. We had a Thanksgiving there."

"Easter. Do you know the back way to the mill?"

In reply he maneuvered his Jeep off Route 100 and followed a circuitous road past grazing horses and spent cornfields. Six years earlier he would have needed her directions to follow the country roads. He looked up through the windshield at the open wingspan of circling hawks. "Will you continue to cut me off every time I make a personal comment, even when we're alone?"

"There's no point in it. You might slip some other time."

"Am I allowed to ask if you're still living out here with your family?"

"I have a place in town, not far from my office. I come out to the family place on weekends or to ride."

"And the rest of the Mendenhalls?"

"River's Edge is still intact. My brother and his wife built a house on the property. My sister's in Boston. My parents have retired and travel a lot now. They're in Maine till the weather turns." Amanda wondered about his own situation, his brother who'd been their best man, his parents in Pittsburgh. He'd mentioned Philadelphia, an hour's commute, but she refused to admit to her curiosity and kept her thoughts to herself.

The deserted millrace covered acreage edging the Brandywine River at one of its dropping points. The rushing water fell over rocks and debris, but once fed a water wheel that provided power to grind grain into flour as early as 1704. The historic significance lay in the fact that the granary had fed and hidden Washington's troops as they fought the Battle of the Brandywine before marching deeper north to Valley Forge.

"The property was bequeathed to the Chadds Ford Historical Society about three years ago," David said.

"I know."

"Right."

It was now marked with small plastic surveyor's flags and rutted by truck tires sunk into the damp ground. David pulled up to the gray fieldstone foundation and turned off the ignition.

The sound of the rushing river replaced the hum of the Jeep as the two of them sat, looking out through the windshield. For no apparent reason his heart began to pound, and his palms moistened as Amanda remained on the seat next to him. He turned to look at her, mildly surprised by what he saw.

"You're blushing, Amanda."

"I'm trying hard not to."

"The memories are sweet, you must admit. What are the chances you gave Marco the bum's rush and took his place so we could rekindle old flames?"

"David . . ." She sighed finally and shook her head. "You can't keep talking like this. You can't treat everything so lightly."

"You're as flushed as the first time you brought me here."

He expected her to rush from the car, but she stayed still. At the hollow of her throat he caught sight of her pulse. The tiny, steady rise and fall of flesh just inside her open collar teased until he had to look away. Was it rapid? Was her breathing shallow? In his chest there was thunder and torment.

"Never mind about the first time."

"Headache?"

"No."

"Marco doesn't know about us and this old place?"

"Of course not." She cleared her throat.

"I hope you had a good laugh when you realized what mill was being restored. I did. I hadn't thought about it in years. Suddenly there was Matt Oakhurst discussing the design and construction of an abandoned flour mill. I wasn't sure it was the same one until I drove out last fall. It was the first I'd been back in Chadds Ford since I don't know when, maybe that last awful Christmas together. I can't remember. I'm not sure I wanted to. You do believe me now that I had no idea you were bidding on the account?"

She seemed to grope for a reply. "Yes. I just want it all put aside. Things were pretty awful at the end."

"Unlike the beginning. What a start, Amanda. It's true what they say about never forgetting the first time."

Next to him she closed her eyes and kept them shut.

A thousand unnamed sensations played in him, not the least of which was a surge of desire just to touch her. He realized then that he hadn't. Except for the initial handshake they'd had no physical contact. He told himself to get out of the car. A jump in the river might help. Moving was beyond him.

"You're embarrassed," he whispered over a quiet laugh. "You were then. So was I, embarrassed and trying so damn hard to be perfect."

Amanda opened her eyes. "David, please don't dredge all that up."

"I'm not dredging. Look at that rock over there, through the windshield. You can't pretend it didn't happen. We lost our virginity in the shelter between that rock and that old mill. It's part of you and part of me. The first time we made love was right here, and that's not so terrible." He pivoted and faced her, his blue eyes warm, his voice suddenly kind.

She shook her head. "It was the beginning of one long mistake. We were so far from perfect for each other. Why on earth did we ever get married?"

"We made that decision right here, too. Why? Because both sets of parents told us not to."

Amanda smiled. "What college sophomores ever listen to their parents?"

They looked into each other's eyes until the moment grew awkward. He watched her. Almost innocently David looked at her mouth, her chin and then back at her exposed throat. He watched her blouse as it rose and fell over erratic breathing. No doubt her pulse was racing. "And because touching you was all I knew of heaven," he whispered.

"David—"

He cocked his head and kissed her once. He pressed his lips perfectly against hers and opened the floodgates to memory, selective memory. The kiss was brief. The yielding stopped. They finished as abruptly as they'd begun. Amanda gulped for air, but David sighed and closed his eyes, then leaned back against the headrest. He listened as she gathered the camera and got out of the car.

David followed and caught up at the mill foundation on the riverbank. She looked overwhelmed. "That was foolish and impetuous. It won't happen again."

"See that it doesn't."

"Just a minute. You started it."

"Started it? I may have been the one reminiscing, but you expected me to kiss you. I suspect you enjoyed it."

Amanda grew incredulous. "Expected? David Smith, I can't even expect decent behavior from you. The last thing on earth I want is to be kissed by you, now, here or any other place." She marched along the bank.

"It seemed the gentlemanly thing to do after I saw the look on your face."

"What look? Don't answer that. You're hallucinating."

"Was I? You changed places with Marco and managed to get out here alone with me."

Amanda rose to the bait like a hungry trout. "You egocentric dreamer. Stop teasing. This isn't funny. This is real life, mine, anyway. You'll always be in never-

never land. I changed places with Marco because we need some shots of the mill. He can't spare the time."

"Dazzle, darling, you may not have come out here to be alone with me, but admit it—you changed places with your partner because you don't trust me. You never did. You think I'm going to spill my guts to your business partner even after six years of barely giving you a second thought. It's time you trusted me, Amanda."

"I can't think of one reason why I should."

"Whether you should or shouldn't is irrelevant. You'll have to. You thought I'd get out here, start laughing with Marco, and tell him about you, about us, over there by the millstone that June."

"It was May," she muttered. "Years ago. A lifetime ago."

"Two lifetimes."

"Don't get wistful on me, David Smith, not after you just insulted me."

"Then don't get hostile. We've shared some memories. We kissed. It was fairly pleasant. Don't blow it out of proportion. Go get your camera. I'm on a tight schedule, too."

Four

The two of them kept to the business at hand. Amanda shot a roll of film as quickly and as professionally as she could. She regretted being dressed in the short, straight skirt and leather shoes, but it wasn't her ensemble that kept her off balance as she scurried over the mill's remains.

David had brought a copy of the plans, and he walked the invisible foundation with her. "Without disturbing the integrity of the existing mill we're going to add a two-story addition here on the north side. It will be totally climate-controlled for archives, containing everything from local documents to period costumes. According to Matt, some Chadds Ford families have historic papers, maps and diaries just waiting for a safe place. The first floor will have one room with a diorama and benches."

"For school groups and tourists," Amanda added. She knew it all from her earlier meetings with the Conservation Council, but the light in David's eyes and the excitement in his voice kept her mostly quiet. That enthusiasm had kept them going as newlyweds the last two years as undergraduates.

He laughed suddenly. "Your eyes are glazing over. I'm boring you."

"No. I was just..." She gathered her thoughts. "I'd forgotten that streak of enthusiasm."

"Reminiscing?"

"Trying not to."

"We had our dreams, you and I."

"It's nice to see that you're designing the kind of projects you always talked about. I heard an awful lot about historic renovation and vernacular design back then."

"All in terms of *someday*."

"*Someday* seems to have arrived. Your parents must be proud of you. They were such worriers, I recall."

"Security above all else. My old man knows nine-to-five, union shops and pension plans. This creative stuff still makes him nervous. To their minds I've failed more than I succeeded."

"You were never the one who failed."

"They thought I failed you, and so did your folks. I was a husband who needed a wife to pay his tuition, then his rent. Who can forget our glorious year in the West Side walk-up?"

Amanda's cheeks flamed. "Maybe it was our expectations that did us in."

"Insight, after all these years?"

"What's the sense of analyzing it? It's over. The divorce was the best thing for both of us, David. We were making each other miserable. Your unhappiness with me affected your work.''

''Doing nothing but drafting other architects' designs affected my work. You married me to prove your parents wrong and divorced me to prove they'd been right.''

''You couldn't get over those blue-collar attitudes about women. You resented every dollar I made, even when it was all we had to live on while you were in grad school.''

''It choked me to accept it from you, but it was worse when your parents offered. There was no way I'd ever take a cent from them. Especially since it was so obvious that it was to make things less miserable for their daughter, whose abject poverty was my fault.''

''I chose the poverty. It was never your fault. At the end—''

David finished for her. ''At the end you were blazing a trail in the advertising world and feeding us both a heck of a lot better than the peanut butter and jelly we started on. I remember, Amanda.''

There was too much to remember. She checked her watch as she railed against her frustration. ''This conversation isn't getting us anywhere. Finish what you were telling me about the mill. I have to get back to the office.''

David's eyes were dark as he once again turned from her to the site. She listened as he talked of repointing the mill's brickwork and replacing the hand-blown panes of glass in the empty window frames.

When had the spark dimmed? When she discovered what a flare she had for advertising? When his long hours in the library and nights at a drawing board were out of balance with her client dinners? When he was still a student, and she was out tasting real life?

If the graduate school years in Princeton had loosened their lovers' knot, their year in Manhattan after graduation had untied it completely. David had joined a huge architectural firm and begun the long, slow road to board certification with the American Institute of Architects.

David pointed at a bank of windows on the blueprints and glanced at her over his reading glasses. "Maybe this would have made a difference, Dazzle. Back then I didn't know what lay ahead. There were no mill restorations, no creative designs."

"Just tedious drafting of someone else's plans for cookie-cutter shopping malls and suburban school buildings. I haven't forgotten."

"My hours were brutal."

"I suppose it didn't seem as if mine were, too. I spent all my extra time soothing your ego, telling you all that effort would pay off, but you had no patience with my Madison Avenue problems."

"They hardly appeared to be problems. I was doing what had to be done. You were doing what you adored. Your whole life revolved around eccentric art directors, clever copywriters and big-budget clients. You made five times what I did and spent it all."

"The wardrobe was as essential as the heat and electricity."

David pulled his glasses off and smiled sardonically. "Even the memories are exhausting. Face it. We were two kids with money problems, fatigue problems, communication problems neither of us had the skill or energy to face. At the end there was so little left to give that we just turned our backs on each other."

"It was the solution."

"Do you ever think there might have been other ways to solve our problems?"

"I try not to think about what's over and done, David. If you don't mind, I need to take those photos." Abruptly Amanda left him and walked to the edge of the foundation. She glanced briefly at the surging river, watched a leaf swirl over the rocks and fought the rising lump in her throat. She'd never failed at anything until she'd failed David. The inability to make him happy had terrified her, until the failure was balanced by professional achievement. Professional success became the salve that had kept them together long after their relationship had sputtered to a standstill. With both families chanting, "We told you so," the chasm between them had become wider than either was able to cross.

"Amanda?"

She blinked as David came around the corner of the building. "I'm glad you're doing what you enjoy," she murmured.

"Thank you." He stayed quiet as she finished shooting a second roll of film.

When he offered his hand, she took it without thinking, then jumped lightly from a low outcropping of rock to the soft earth. She watched him look at her naked ring finger before he let go. "You shouldn't have kissed me."

He nodded. "Stirred up a hornets' nest of memories, just the way this old place does. There's no denying we were madly in love. Then, anyway."

"Or thought we were."

"It seemed real in the beginning."

"Everything does, in the beginning."

"We had our own lives to work out. We never should have fouled things up by thinking our relationship was anything more than physical attraction. Our families tried to tell us. You did, too, after it was too late. I was too working-class for your family. I didn't belong in Ivy League schools I couldn't afford. Nobody wanted you trading Mendenhall for Smith."

"I was too upper-class for yours. They thought I'd corrupt you, make you a snob, and you'd turn your back on them."

"They were wrong," David said quietly.

"So were mine," she added, confused by the softness of David's reply. Amanda's pulse raced. They spoke over the babbling of the Brandywine, watching the water instead of each other.

"The mistakes were deeper than our social backgrounds."

"So was the hurt. It's amazing what two people can do to each other." David threw a rock into the water. "You were meant for this. Your own agency on your home turf agrees with you. It's good to see all that hard work has paid off."

She fought the compliment as the mood changed. "You hated all that hard work."

"There's no denying I hated the hours you kept. When I think about our marriage—which isn't often, believe me—I honestly don't think of us together much."

"I put you through graduate school, David. That can't be done by staying in an apartment all day."

"It wasn't the days."

"Those troubled nights were a reflection of how our days had gone. We were too young. We made each other miserable. We've gone on with our lives."

Amanda turned from the riverbank and busied herself with the camera. Without another comment she got back into the Jeep.

David took the main route back—no more meandering country roads. The return ride was electric with unspoken conversation. He forced himself to concentrate on the road and listen to the radio. He was angry with himself for the wistful moments and a little ashamed at the need to dredge up her biggest failure.

When he double-parked in front of Mendenhall and Lipton, Amanda thanked him. "Don't come in. There's no reason."

"I wasn't planning to." He kept his hands on the steering wheel but looked into her eyes. "Has it been all empire building these six years?"

"We've gotten much too personal already."

"You make me curious. You were always an enigma. One last question."

"All right, one."

"Was there anybody in Seattle? Did you ever come close a second time?"

"David, the less we rehash the past, the better off you and I will be. This isn't the time or place for intimate questions."

He smiled. "I'll wait."

"You mustn't. All this curiosity is a waste of time."

"It's healthy, curiosity. You're curious, too, and sooner or later you'll ask. For all you know I have a loving wife and beautiful children now." His heart leaped at the shock in her expression.

"Do you?"

"Would you care?"

"Never mind. I won't play your game. What you've done with your life—every aspect of it—is none of my business."

"You were lost in thought back there at the mill."

"Never mind about the mill."

"Tell me about your dinner companion last night. I've been wondering."

"Don't wonder."

"After the way you and I lived, it's hard to imagine you in a purely social situation. I see you in a black cocktail dress making deals over the pâté."

She looked both exasperated and hurt. "I took the president of a car dealership to dinner. We discussed a six-month retainer for radio and television spots. I made him a proposal."

"Indecent, I hope." He waited, well aware of his ability to manipulate her emotions. She seemed stung, amused and infuriated. She tried not to laugh and covered her face with her hands.

"Six years have improved you, Dazzle."

"Don't bait me. I have no intention of responding."

"Then so long, and good luck on your golden path."

"Your path hasn't been golden, too?"

"Are you asking?"

"No. What you've done these past years is none of my business. Goodbye, David."

He shrugged. "I can't leave until you get out of the car, and you'd better scoot out now before I submit to this urge to kiss you again."

"What have I done to deserve this?"

"Quite simply, you married me, drove me crazy, divorced me and went blithely along your golden path without me. It's got me curious as hell."

Five

Amanda threw down her pencil and glared at Marco as he knocked, opened the door and entered her office hours later. "I told Karen no interruptions. Go away. I'm working. You should be, too."

His tie was off and his shirt open at the neck. The sleeves were rolled up to his forearms. "Look at me. I'm undressed for working. Of course, I'd rather be undressed for fooling around."

Amanda remained stone faced.

"My sexist comments usually get a snappy come-back. May we assume this mood will prevail as long as you're preparing the Oakhurst account?"

"Why is it that men assume so much in the first place?"

"Men. Do you mean male architects and their assumptions? How about ex-husbands and their assumptions?"

"At the moment I mean art directors and their assumptions."

Marco nodded. "I, for one, assume there's a lot of bitterness and resentment between you and David." He put his fist to his heart. "Try as you might, you can't ignore all those little crumbs swept under the proverbial rug. Neither can he."

"Do your job, Marco, and stop assuming."

He dropped a magnifying glass and the freshly developed spec sheet from her morning photo session onto her desk. "Your disposition's worse than I thought. I am doing my job. Here's proof."

She groaned at the pun and picked them up. "I'm sorry. Thank you." Amanda took the glass and looked over the sheet. She studied it carefully and noted in the margins what she hoped to use. When she finished, she raised her head. "You're still here."

"We have work to do, remember? Let's talk about the layout, since I've already interrupted you."

She was relieved. "All right, Marco. Can you use a before-and-after format for the brochure? This is a nice clear shot of the mill."

"Sure." He took back the sheet and picked up the magnifying glass. "I thought I might find at least one shot with your architect in it."

"Business, D'Abruzzi. He's not *my* architect. Even when we were married, he wasn't my architect."

Marco arched his eyebrows. "Now there's a clue to your failed relationship and hidden past."

"No clues. Your position with this agency is hanging by a thread. Go back to your drawing board."

"I'm Italian. I have to ask. No heart-to-hearts this morning? I thought you might have accomplished something more than new business, maybe some old, unfinished business."

"That doesn't deserve a reply, but for your information our old business is finished. It was finished in civil court, complete with attorneys. What you see on that sheet is what we accomplished this morning." She pointed to her open door. "Out."

Marco sat in the empty chair instead. "Amanda, is it worth the agony? The Oakhurst project isn't a life-or-death financial break for us. We've got some big accounts, and there'll be plenty more with our reputation. We're successful, you pay me every week, payroll's stable. Chuck this, kid, and go after something that doesn't have your ex-husband attached to it."

Amanda stood and stared across the desk. "Stop looking at me like a lost puppy. My ex-husband will have no bearing on this account."

Marco stood and stared right back at her. "You're lying to a man you spend fourteen hours a day with. I'm the closest you've got to a best friend, and I know you better than you know yourself." He sighed, his expression pure sympathy. "Name one artist who can keep her—or his—professional life removed from emotion, especially love."

"This is hardly love, Marco!"

"Hate?"

"Of course it isn't hate. We're civilized adults. The fact that David has suddenly shown up right under my nose threw me a little, that's all. I'd like to think it falls somewhere between the two, in some nice, neutral, unemotional pocket of my life and David's."

"Your life doesn't have nice, neutral, unemotional pockets. You're a copywriter and account executive.

You're volatile. You'd make a great Neapolitan. It goes with the territory."

Amanda walked the width of the room. "Marco, I want to prepare this presentation for the mill project as smoothly as possible. I want it polished, I want it professional and I want it over. It's unfortunate that I have to see David occasionally and that it's his design. I'm dealing with it the best way I know how, and I don't want to dwell on him." She stopped and looked at Marco. "If you value your life, you'll stop bringing up his name every time you get within five feet of me."

"You need my help."

"I intend to have the rough copy for the covering brochure ready by the end of the day. I need your help for the design. The design, Marco. *Comprendo?*"

"*Capeesh* is the word you want."

"*Yes, boss* are the words I want! I'll block in roughs for the photos and sketches. This is an educational giveaway. Two panel, one color. By tomorrow I want you to rough out the more-detailed booklet that will be distributed from the museum to students and visitors."

Marco stood up and saluted. "How the woman can change the subject. I understand everything. You can count on me."

They both looked at Karen as she entered the office. "I tried to keep him out, but he never listens to me. Marco, you have a phone call from Oakhurst Design Group. Amanda, I was just wondering, do you need anything delivered to that architectural firm? I could return those blueprints or something to David Smith."

Marco put his arm across Karen's shoulders as they left the room. "Let's talk conflict of interest for a minute. Besides, I think he's married, two kids, gorgeous wife.''

Amanda's heart jumped.

Marco closed her door without looking back.

At 9:00 p.m. David parked his sports car at the curb of the unfamiliar city block. In the lamplight he scanned the neat row of bow-front houses, relieved that the one he was searching for still had lights glowing. He raised the brass knocker and rapped, then waited. Above him a curtain parted. He waved at the figure.

"What are you doing here at this time of night?" she called down.

"May I come in?"

"Certainly not."

He knocked again as the old adrenaline began to pump. All afternoon he'd been denying the chemistry that obviously still percolated. He was still telling himself it was strictly business when the door opened a crack.

"This is totally uncalled-for," Amanda said from the sliver of interior light at the doorframe. Crimson satin peeked from the collar of what appeared to be a winter coat. "It's far too late for coming in, and you don't belong here."

He waved the manila envelope he was carrying. "I had a heck of a time finding the house, but I saw a light on. Boss's orders, I promise."

"Matthew Oakhurst?"

"None other." My God, he thought, it had been years since his body had dictated behavior. The pull was as strong as those first weeks on campus when he was driven by the challenge in her eyes, and his own audacity.

"Make it quick." She opened the door but made no effort to welcome him.

The spring in his chest tightened, but he laughed. Amanda stood in front of him in a down-filled, calf-length winter coat. Her legs and feet were bare. "I know the weather's cooling down, but isn't that outerwear a little heavy for tonight? You forgot your fur-lined boots."

"Cute." Amanda took the envelope with one hand and held the coat closed at her breastbone with the other. "I got ready for bed early."

He flushed and glanced at the staircase. "Am I interrupting?"

"Your presence in this city is an interruption. Go home. If whatever's in this envelope isn't self-explanatory, I'll call you in the morning."

"That's why I'm here. I'll be out at a site in Philadelphia for the next two days on a project."

"You have a comeback for every single thing I say!"

"Forgive me. When you tell me you'll call in the morning, I feel obligated to reply that I won't be there."

"Then come in, damn it."

"Come in, damn it, will have to do." David smiled as if she'd warmly welcomed him, and followed her into the living room. "If you're entertaining someone, I'll just be a minute."

"David Smith, you'll just be a minute, regardless."

"Are you?"

"It's none of your business." Amanda crossed the room. "No," she added softly.

He was hiding behind repartee and he knew it. He hadn't expected the excitement to sink so deep, hadn't expected forgotten moments to spring into his brain every time he looked at her. He hadn't expected the pain.

"Well?"

He glanced around the room and recognized half a dozen objects. Could she tell he was remembering? A calico cat trotted across the room and rubbed itself against Amanda's legs. David knelt. "You must be Lipton, the elusive advertising executive." When he tried to scoop it into his arms, however, the cat scurried away with a howl of protest and disappeared back the way it had come. "About as fond of me as your business partner," he called after it.

"David—"

He stepped to the coffee table and picked up a brass candlestick. "This was a wedding present."

"We divided the community property. This isn't the time to take inventory. Make this quick. I have work to do, and I'm beastly hot in this coat."

"Take it off. Impure thoughts are the farthest thing from my mind."

She let go of the lapels and left it unbuttoned but still on, then self-consciously touched her hair. "I look awful. I was hardly expecting company."

His own sense of relief annoyed him. "You're incapable of looking awful."

She paused, then murmured, "Thank you."

"You're welcome. As I recall, you weren't much good at thank-yous." Before she could reply he cocked his head. "That's the robe, isn't it?"

She made a pretense of glancing at what she had on. "Yes."

The robe. She still had the peignoir set he'd spent every last dime on for their first anniversary. Desire was like a sudden kick in the ribs. He sucked in a breath and forced himself to open the envelope.

"Matthew and I had a dinner meeting with Wilkins and the Conservation Council tonight." He pulled on his glasses from his breast pocket and skimmed the print as he showed her the contents of the envelope. "This is their description of the museum, what it will offer, program development, stuff like that. There's also some background on the Battle of the Brandywine and Washington's troops. I told them I'd see that you got it."

"I hope you didn't say you'd give it to me at my house in the middle of the night."

"It's not the middle of the night."

"Did you?"

David jammed both hands into his pockets. "I said I'd swing by and drop it off, if you were still up. If I were Oakhurst, you wouldn't think a thing about it."

"You're not Oakhurst, David. You're my ex-husband."

"I do believe that's the first time I've heard you use the term."

"I'm sorry it applies."

David stared at her without reply. She looked apologetic, defiant and just short of overwhelmed. There was no doubt that she was as confused by the circumstances as he was. It did terrible things to his libido.

"Surprising neighborhood," he said at last. "Multiethnic, multiracial, blue-collar is a big step for you. Some attitudes have changed in six years."

"I have lovely neighbors. It's safe, and I'm happy here. I assume you've changed a little in six years, too, although I haven't seen much evidence."

"Professionally I don't struggle as hard. The early work paid off. I have you to thank for that."

"Why is it that you bait me, toss insults and innuendos, and then just when I want to wring your neck, you say something half-pleasant about me?"

"Because running into you has turned me inside out. I have this gnawing need to keep you off balance, too." They stood in front of the couch. Knowing she'd never offer, David put his glasses back into his pocket and sat. He tugged her wrist and pulled her down next to him. "I suspect under all this fear and bitterness you're trying to make sense of long-buried, not entirely welcome emotions."

"I'm not."

"Well, I am."

Six

"Why can't you have the decency to keep your honesty to yourself? This is no time to start analyzing our mutual misery."

"Or worse, our mutual joy?" David smiled at her, buoyed by her doubt. "Memories die more slowly than I ever imagined, good ones and bad."

"If I seem bitter, you can hardly blame me. Your presence makes everything doubly hard. Things have been going so well. Marco and I have knocked ourselves out to get to this point."

"You never resented a challenge."

"I resent the fact that you make this harder than it has to be." She sighed heavily and looked at the brass candlestick on the coffee table at her knees.

"Your fear is unnecessary, Amanda."

"I'm not afraid of you. I'm afraid of our past jeopardizing my future."

David picked up the candlestick. He turned it in his hands, and it made his heart leap. With just the single flame of that little candle there had been nights when they were convinced their passion was all the foundation their marriage had needed. There had been nights of nothing but love and conversation that had stretched till dawn. Nights when she . . .

Amanda took the candlestick and put it back on the table.

It was time to put her at ease. "Our past is a scapegoat. No one concerned with this account has any idea, not that Matt would care. I doubt anybody would care. Have you told anyone in your family that we've run into each other?"

"No."

"Idle gossip might travel."

"My parents are in Maine. My brother and sister lead their own lives."

He leaned back against the couch. "How is Scott? His kids must be grown-up. And Lisa?"

"Fine, happily married, settled. David, it's time to go home."

He leaned forward, elbows propped on his knees. "All right, but as long as I'm here tonight I might as well take the blame for this mess you think you're in, although I swear I had no more idea than you did about anything."

"I'm not looking for someone to blame. We're beyond the blaming stage," Amanda replied quietly.

"When this is over, I'd like to get on with my life, too. Has it occurred to you that if we settle things between us, we'll both be happier?"

"That's what the divorce was for."

"That's what I thought, but it was too easy. It made it possible to walk away without resolving anything."

"Nothing was resolvable! The divorce gave us a chance to put that life behind us, a clean break." She closed her eyes and looked genuinely exhausted.

"There was nothing clean about it."

"Don't add any more stress."

"This isn't all fun and games for me, either. I know I'm playing with fire. I thought I wanted to forget everything as much as you do, but the sorry truth is, every time I see you, every time I touch something like this candlestick, a lifetime of memories shoves reality aside."

"The reality is that we were poison for each other."

"Then keep repeating it. I'm searching for my equilibrium, Dazzle, just as you are. Poison. I told myself that when I was nineteen, but it didn't do any good. I didn't know then how deep hurt could go, how much damage two people can do to each other."

"And now we both know."

"No matter what you think, I've grown up, too. I'd like to think we can be friends. It's a risk, but it might prove that the damage we did to each other wasn't permanent."

She put her head back. "Maybe, after a while, but you'd probably regret it all over again. Marco tells me I push friends aside. I don't mean to. It just happens."

He sat on the edge of the cushion and looked at her. There was warmth in her eyes, beautiful eyes full of life, which had been such a magnet. There was curiosity, too, and a wariness, which hurt to look at now.

"Marco's a supportive, nonthreatening refuge from the rest of your world."

"In some ways I love Marco dearly. We're business partners, creative links in a soldered chain. Good art directors who can put up with me are hard to find. I'm lousy at personal relationships, but I'm a good business partner." She grew pensive. "I don't know whether it matters to you, David, but I want you to know that I've never blamed anything on you. I've always said it was mutual."

"It was mutual, but not so much that it should have kept you from finding someone else."

"Business relationships are complicated enough."

"And you've become the quintessential career woman."

"I should have stuck to this career stuff all along. I love it. I'm a damn good account executive. We need the Oakhurst account. It would let us take off financially, which will affect us creatively. We desperately need a full-time copywriter so I can devote my time to administering the accounts and Marco can stick to design. What little extra we have covers a part-time bookkeeper/accountant. I want to grow just enough to make an impact in this town."

"You do make an impact."

"Thank you."

He got up from the couch with her. He ached with melancholy, as heavy as the coat Amanda pulled closed again. He longed to kiss her and fought the desire with every fiber in him.

The moment dragged painfully. Finally Amanda said, "You'd better go."

"I know."

He took another look around the understated room. "I like your taste, and I admire your values." Small talk.

"A pleasant surprise?" she asked as she opened the front door.

"No, just things I'd forgotten." This was the moment, and he remembered the look, the deepening of those tepid eyes, the flush across her cheeks. Memory sent his blood surging, racing as he reached out and touched her hair.

"Good night, David," she whispered to him.

He looked at his palms. How many times had he slid his hands under her coat, found her willing, eager to welcome him? It was too long ago, heartaches ago. His face was aflame with the memory of it and so was hers.

David moved first and tucked one of her lapels under the other. "Good night," he repeated, and walked through the open door into the lamplight. No kiss.

"*Do* you have children and a wife waiting?"

He turned on the stoop. "I'm better at business relationships, too." He studied her.

"Stop flirting with me."

"I wish to hell I could." He pulled his car keys and glasses from his pockets and turned to the quiet street. "You do dazzle, Amanda, especially when you try not to remember what I'm suddenly trying not to forget."

Though Amanda wasn't about to admit it to anyone, the evening visit from David eased some unconscious anxiety. Her mood lightened once her pulse slowed. She hung her coat in the closet, then went back upstairs to her office and finished her work with a clear head.

She accepted her attraction to him and attributed it to the shock of the ludicrous reunion they found themselves part of. She felt sure it would fade as it had the last time—with reality. For the first time in hours the thought of him didn't constantly interrupt her concentration.

She'd spent six years fighting ghosts, six years trying to forget how she'd failed the one person she'd wanted desperately to please. She doubted that they could ever be friends, but if she left well enough alone, perhaps they would no longer be enemies.

And for the time being, leaving well enough alone was easy. Knowing David was away for two days and not about to march into Mendenhall and Lipton did wonders for her productivity. Her old spirit revived. She matched Marco in energy, and they put every spare minute into creating the roughs for the campaign. David neither showed up nor called for the rest of the week.

Marco slouched in her office chair at four o'clock on Friday, grinning broadly. "You haven't thrown me out of here in days."

"You're working hard, Marco. Even Toys Galore is happy."

"You noticed. How encouraging. The old adrenaline settling down? Things kind of kicked into high gear when the architect dropped back into your life."

"What things?" she demanded.

He shrugged and gestured at the air. "Defenses, emotional instability, irritability."

"You may stop now, D'Abruzzi."

"I will. I don't think he means you any harm, Amanda. I'd be on his case in a flash if I did."

"Am I supposed to thank you for that unnecessary chivalry?"

He grinned. "If you like."

She smiled back. "As a thank-you, how about a date a week from Saturday night?"

Marco narrowed his gaze. "Too easy. I know your tricks. Would this date have anything to do with the Gold Ballroom of the Hotel DuPont?"

"Maybe. What it really has to do with is scholarship money."

"Amanda, you can't drag me to that black-tie Advertising Council thing."

"It's not a *thing*. It's the annual dinner dance, a fund-raiser for scholarships. Everybody in the business goes. You know that. It does a lot of good. It's necessary to your career as well as mine, and it can be fun."

"Nothing black-tie can be fun."

"You didn't go last year, so how would you know?"

"I had the flu. Sort of."

"The flu had long blond hair, as I recall."

"She was a homebody. We didn't feel like going out."

"Well, next Saturday will be less fun than the blonde, more fun than the flu. You'll see."

"Do I have to dance?"

"Only if you're not drumming up business and networking."

He pretended to look thoughtful. "I suppose you'll wear something slinky and wonderful?"

"Nothing to incite, Marco, dear."

"Rats. Still, it is a real date with one gorgeous woman."

Amanda laughed. "May I count on you?"

"Anything for Mendenhall and Lipton."

"Good. I'll hold you to it. Now go home and enjoy the weekend."

Marco got out of the chair and paused at the door. "If I told you to do the same thing, would you?"

"Yes. I haven't been to the farm in weeks. Maybe I'll drive out."

"Just you and the horses," he scoffed.

"They can be more pleasant than human company."

Seven

Amanda got both Marco and Karen out of the office by five o'clock, then put in another half hour. She filled her portfolio with the rough storyboards Marco had prepared for the Oakhurst presentation, and her briefcase with the copies of the blueprints for the mill. She also had to proofread a printer's galley for a merchant's sidewalk sale she'd arranged for a mall account.

All of it went onto the passenger seat of her car. When she got back to her duplex, she threw casual clothes together for the weekend, and by six o'clock she and Lipton were heading north on the Kennett Pike. She passed the entrance to the Winterthur Museum and turned off into the bucolic back lanes of Centerville, over the state line and finally into the rolling hills of Chadds Ford, Pennsylvania, and what she still considered home.

Dusk settled as she navigated Route 100 in her sports car. She slowed at the vacant mill site and looked at the tiny surveyor's markers as they flapped in the deepening light. She hadn't seen David in days. She stared at the ruins, feeling no frustration, no anxiety, no regret, no confusing physical pull she refused to call desire.

There was only confidence, the old spark and sure knowledge that, if she were just left alone, Mendenhall and Lipton could do a superb job for the Conservation Council.

River's Edge was the euphemistic term four generations of Mendenhalls used for their property, which bordered the Brandywine River as it rushed over the state line from Pennsylvania into Delaware. The original fieldstone manse, built as a country retreat and working farm, had been a forty-five-minute trip by private railroad car in 1870. The Mendenhalls at first came out for a respite from city life in Wilmington for the pastoral solitude of grazing horses and country air.

More than one hundred and twenty years later, Amanda's branch of the family and the retainers who kept it all in working order still maintained it lovingly. Amanda was in the enviable position of having River's Edge at her disposal; it took only a last-minute phone call.

She got out of her car and cleared David from her thoughts. After the five-day headache that had been her workweek, the rewards she felt she deserved were two days of solitude, a hot bath and home-cooked meals. Reverie, regret and remorse weren't on her agenda.

The house smelled wonderfully of the season's final flowers, arranged in hallways and on end tables as if ten people were in residence. In the kitchen Amanda put Lipton down, hugged Hannah Jimerson, the housekeeper, and asked for dinner in the study after her bath. She took her things upstairs and unpacked in the front bedroom. It was the same room where she'd grown up, the one in which David Smith had kissed her senseless when he came home as her guest. It was the room she'd shared with her young husband on school holidays, and the one she'd used when she found herself single again at the tender age of twenty-five.

Amanda's mood was bright, her mind on business. She soaked luxuriously in the tub, then went back downstairs to the cozy, book-lined room at the end of the front hall. She settled in her crimson dressing gown with the printer's galley and a glass of sherry.

At eight o'clock Hannah brought Amanda a light supper, insisting that she was delighted to have someone to cook for, then left for her own quarters, which she shared with her husband, who managed the stables and grounds. Amanda finished her supper and got back to her work when she was momentarily startled by sounds at the front door.

A male voice called, "Hannah?"

"Scott?" Amanda called back. "It's Amanda. I'm in the library."

"Amanda? No kidding!"

Too late she realized her brother was speaking to someone else, as well. When she couldn't find an afghan or throw to put around her shoulders, she stood and turned for the back stairs. However, Scott's voice sounded again, this time from the doorway.

"Amanda, what the blazes are you doing here?"

She stood, clutched the galleys to her breasts and turned the color of her dressing gown. Scott Mendenhall, still in protective leather chaps, was in stocking feet, holding shin-high riding boots. David Smith, once again as flushed as she, stood next to him in his socks. He held unlaced gum-soled boots.

"Hello, Amanda."

"David."

Scott looked from one to the other expectantly.

As Amanda regained her composure, she frowned. "Damn it, David, you'd better have a darn good explanation for this one." She again looked for something to wrap around her.

"Allow me," David replied. He put down the boots and backtracked to the front closet. Without a word he returned and offered an open man's fleece-lined hunting jacket.

"Really," she muttered.

"You'll be more comfortable," he insisted, then grinned as she shot her arms into the sleeves.

"I had no idea." Scott looked from his sister, now wrapped in crimson satin and olive drab, to his former brother-in-law. "Why do I get the feeling you've seen each other since the courtroom drama six years ago?"

"He hasn't told you?"

"You didn't want anyone to know," David replied.

Scott looked at the two of them again. "David, when I mentioned Amanda's agency not half an hour ago, you told me you thought she was in Seattle."

David shrugged. "I lied. Please give me credit for that, Amanda. The truth is, Scott, your sister and her cat are bidding on the mill restoration I designed for the Conservation Council. I pretended not to know she was back because she—Amanda, not Lipton—has a deathly fear that the council or contractors or architects will find out we were married."

"Nepotism," Scott remarked.

"See, Scott agrees with me," Amanda added.

"Not entirely. I wasn't aware you were even speaking to each other."

"She's doing her best not to," David replied.

Scott, older than his sister by three years, patted her shoulder. "Fine. Go back to your office work. You'll never know he's here."

"Here? In this house? Don't be insane. David, what are you doing?"

David had the audacity to sit on the arm of the couch. "It's pure coincidence. Since I'm now working in the Oakhurst Wilmington office as well as Philadelphia, I thought something out here in the country, halfway between the two, would be nice. I found a rental at the Lydons' place—Sycamore Hill, right around the bend. Just to set the record straight, I made the appointment to look at it well before you waltzed back into my life."

"I have not waltzed back into your life."

"He's renting a carriage house," Scott added. "I was on the tennis court with Jace Lydon when David showed up with the rental agent. Small world."

"Shrinking, even as we speak," Amanda added.

"Stop scowling."

"I suppose Scott dragged you over here the minute you signed the lease."

"No, that was yesterday. Your brother talked me into coming out this afternoon."

"And getting on a horse and spending the night?" Amanda looked at them both incredulously.

"Afraid so, Sis. We went riding before dark. We've been walking the back slope. I showed him my place, introduced him to the kids. Time got away from us, so we've just come over to square things with Hannah."

"Lots of memories out here," David added.

"Never mind the memories. If you're really staying, I'm going back to town. David, you can have any room you want." She picked up her papers as the men stepped back to let her by. Scott put his hand on David's shoulder, but otherwise, to her surprise, neither man tried to stop her as she climbed the stars to her room.

David looked quickly at Scott. "Wait here." He put down his boots and climbed the stairs in his socks. Amanda was at her dresser. The hunting jacket lay in a heap on the bed, and she held a pair of jeans in her arms.

The bedside lamplight cast her shadow on the irregular horsehair plaster wall. For a long, painful moment he looked at her silhouette.

"You think I'm being childish," she said.

He raised his eyebrows.

"You don't approve of my behavior. I can feel it. I could always feel it."

Frustration, so often a painful wedge between them, rose in him. This time David was grave, his voice low and level. "Amanda, you don't honestly want me to speculate on what I think you feel underneath those thin layers of satin, do you? Never mind. I don't know what you feel. Sometimes I think I never did."

"Does what I want matter at all?"

"Yes."

"The visit to my house in town was one thing, but this! You know how important it is that we stay apart. This whole thing is a joke to you."

He cleared his throat. "Quite the contrary. I'm taking this very seriously. I had no idea you'd be here."

"Even without me, it's my family."

"I have to be back downtown at nine in the morning. Scott simply thought it would save the commute up to Philadelphia and back if I stayed over. We had no idea you'd be here. If anyone goes, it should be me."

"Fine, I agree," Amanda said.

"Before I do, give me one straight answer. What's really bothering you? Besides the fact that this fifteen-room house isn't big enough for both of us, and I jeopardize your business chances, is there anything else?"

"No."

"Good. I thought you might have been embarrassed that for the second time in a week I've found you in the gown I gave you for our first anniversary."

"I've hardly worn it—"

"One of the most unforgettable nights of our brief, bittersweet marriage," he continued.

"David" came out in a breathy plea. She threw her jeans at him, but there was no rage in her expression, just confusion. She stepped toward him, and his body responded instantly.

"Oh, Dazzle," he whispered. "The memory is torture, but the pain is sweet."

Eight

Desire worked its dangerous magic on every fiber of Amanda's body as she stood with the bed between them. Then without another word—or appraising glance—David dropped her jeans onto the mattress and left the room. Through the open window she heard him leave the house.

Scott's voice drifted as they stood below, putting on their boots. "Is she still giving you a hard time?"

"I wouldn't recognize her if she weren't," David replied as they crossed the flagstone terrace and walked into the night.

By seven Saturday morning Amanda was the antithesis of the way she'd appeared Friday night. Dressed in jeans and a wool sweater, she hurried through cereal and toast and then left Lipton and headed for the stables, which opened at the edge of the pasture on the north side of the property. She sipped a mug of steaming coffee as she walked down the lane.

Amanda forced herself to concentrate on the spectacular views and the crisp morning. Strong, physical labor would help. It always did. She greeted Hank Jimerson as she passed him. The farm manager had already put the horses, which had been stabled for the night, out to graze.

She exchanged her gum-soled shoes for riding boots in the tack room, found a pitchfork and set to mucking out the stalls. She forked and lifted the old hay and manure and carried it to the courtyard, where she pitched it into the back of the farm's tractor wagon. A barn swallow shot from the rafters.

As Amanda shifted her forkload into the hay wagon, she watched the darting bird and caught sight of a figure coming up the cart path. She stood still and watched, not daring to put a name to the unwelcome pleasure she felt.

His gait was familiar, the tilt of his head recognizable. The horses loped toward the fence as he passed, but he didn't stop for them. He didn't stop until he came into the courtyard and up to the tractor.

He was in jeans, newer than hers, and a clean flannel shirt. Both hands were in his pockets, which bunched the hem of an old tweed sport jacket he wore over the shirt. She recognized the jacket.

His long, confident strides put spring in his step and speed in her pulse. He wore clothes well. He looked just as good without them.

She sucked in a breath. Where had *that* thought come from? His height made him physically striking. She looked at his hair, his April blue eyes, the curve of his thigh, then damned him, damned the regret that teased her. There was nothing to be gained by any of this. She was breathing too hard, too aware of the thumping under her thick sweater and the moistness in her hands as she leaned the pitchfork against the tractor wheel.

"I thought I'd find you here. Sleep well?" David asked as he came to her.

"Not particularly."

He looked at the stalls. "Funny feeling, being out last evening with Scott and the horses."

"So I would think. I thought you went home last night."

"Nope, I stayed with your brother." He put up his hands. "Before you start in on me again, I know what your philosophy is. I'm intruding on your territory. You don't want me to have anything more to do with Scott than with Marco or your receptionist."

"David, I gave you good reasons for my feelings. Now you're renting the carriage house around the bend. The Lydons are very good friends of ours."

"Have you forgotten that I was the guest of honor at the party they gave for us after we eloped?"

"I guess I did."

He pivoted and looked out at the hills, but made no effort to leave. "Beautiful morning for a ride. Leaves will be turning soon."

"Yes," she replied. "I'm going out by myself."

She waited and he turned back to her. "Amanda?" They looked at each other again. Neither one smiled. "I came over here this morning to apologize. I'm sorry about last night. Seeing you in that dressing gown, twice in one week—" A smile played at the corners of his mouth.

"Was just too much to let pass?"

"Yes. Some things I'll never forget. Some memories just don't quit."

"That's all they are, memories, *selective* memories."

"Can you admit that our years together weren't all bad?"

She picked up the pitchfork. "Of course. Now, if you'll excuse me, I have stalls to clean."

"You'll always find something to hide behind."

She bridled. "Naturally there were good times. The mistake was marrying, thinking there could be more than just some big, dumb crush. We grew apart, David, very quickly. You hated my work."

"I didn't understand it."

"It doesn't matter now."

"It matters, Amanda, it matters. All of a sudden it's in the way, like thick cobwebs I've got to sweep aside. I could pretend it didn't when you were three thousand miles away. But now? It won't stay under the rug any longer."

"Don't spoil the happiness and success we have now."

"I won't. Just give me time to remember why I don't love you anymore."

It was a good exit line, but this time David couldn't force himself to turn and leave. Surprise widened her eyes again, and again he welcomed the thunder in his chest. No other woman exasperated him, tortured him, or made him feel more alive. She was still a challenge, still an enigma, still a mirror of early dreams.

Instinct drove him where common sense evaporated. He began to think in similes. She was as skittish as a colt. Maybe he was courting disaster, but there was only one way to find out.

She went back to work with the pitchfork. "I'm selfish, independent and single-minded."

"Those are the things I loved about you."

"You want hay down your back?"

Where was her anger? She stood in front of him, obviously expecting him to stomp off into the morning. Instead he stayed at the tractor. She smelled, even over the hay and horse sweat, of herbal shampoo and cologne. Six years and she was still using the same scents.

"What did you love about me?" he asked as he pulled a stray piece of hay from her hair. "There must have been something." Careful, *be careful*.

She sighed. "Your talent. Your dreams. I loved your designs. I've told you that already, at the mill." Without looking at him she asked, "Was I really so selfish?"

"It was your description, not mine. Independent and single-minded ring true, however."

"For you, as well, David. You mustn't call what we had love. It was more like a crush."

"A crush, and it crushed both of us, all that flirting and sighing and dreaming. There were plenty of good times. You in that satin. Every once in a while, on a cold night, I'm sure you think about me in those pajamas."

"You never wore pajamas."

"Gotcha!" He laughed.

"I thought you said you'd grown up."

"This is an adult game. I may not be serious enough for your liking, but the former Amanda Mendenhall Smith needs a dose of loosening up. Stop taking your job, your life, our *former* relationship so damn seriously."

She turned from him and went to the next stall, then shoved the pitchfork deep into the matted hay as he came beside her. "If you have business in Wilmington this morning, you really shouldn't show up smelling like horses. Please move."

He stepped back. "I am moving. This is it for a while. I just didn't want more hard feelings between us. I want to make sure I can recognize the difference between love and a crush next time."

"I don't want to stand here and discuss next time, love or crushes with my ex-husband. We both made a mistake, we both have faults. That's why we were divorced."

The light made her eyes smoky and fathomless as she waited for his reply. Go easy, he told himself. She began to turn. "I never meant to hurt you, Amanda."

She stopped. "David, I . . . please. It's forgotten. *Everything is forgotten.*" Her voice trembled. "You didn't hurt me."

"I did, but it was pride, stubborn pride." He cupped her cheek with his palm and savored the heat under his fingers as desire danced through him. "Forgive me. I want to be free of this as much as you do." Before she could turn away he dropped his hand.

"There's nothing to forgive. You are free, if you'd just leave all of this alone." Her voice was thick. "Please leave."

As abruptly as he'd started, he quit. With the self-control of a Spartan he shoved both hands into his pockets and nodded. "Good advice. It's about time I listened. I'm leaving you alone, meant to all along. That's what I came over to tell you. Good luck with the campaign. I wish you all the best, Amanda, truly."

*   *   *

He turned and started away so quickly that Amanda was startled. She watched briefly, kicked the tractor tire and returned to the stall. Her body was humming, yet she could feel herself being manipulated. She pressed a fist against her racing heart, hating him for upsetting the fine balance she'd finally brought to her life. There had never been a balance where David Smith was concerned, never been common sense or clearheadedness.

All she could remember was emotion, deep, surging, engulfing emotion. Ecstasy and misery, bliss and frustration were all buried. She wanted nothing more than what she had at the moment—contentment.

She stole a final glance at him as he walked the cart path to her brother's house. Long ago she'd taken back all that she'd given him. Her cheek suddenly tingled where he'd touched her. She rubbed the back of her hand across it and marched to the tack room.

Amanda spent the morning on horseback. She startled deer, raised a covey of partridges and tore over the open hillside. For hours she never saw another human and never felt the need. Astride her mare, she focused on her happy childhood, the success of her career, the assignments ahead of her. By the time she returned the saddle to its brace in the tack room and hung up the bridle, she'd mentally rearranged the format for the Oakhurst brochure. By the time she groomed her horse and put the animal back out to pasture, Amanda's mental agenda was as crowded as any workweek. Work was the cure. It always had been.

As she brushed back her hair, a piece of hay came away in her fingers. Her cheek tingled again. Her heart raced. "You have no right to do this to me," she whispered, her throat tight. "You have no right."

Nine

On Monday morning there was nothing to be gained by telling Marco of the Friday night incident, nor were there any business reasons for David Smith to show up at Mendenhall and Lipton. Nevertheless, her concentration was continually broken by expectation. Every encounter with David had been unexpected. Consequently every odd footstep, any male voice in the outer office, the slamming of a door sent her heart to her throat.

She spent the week preparing for the Oakhurst presentation, in addition to meeting regular deadlines. Neither she nor Marco left before eight at night, and Karen often stayed long enough to get them pizza or Chinese take-out dinners.

"Brilliant as usual," Marco declared the following Friday at lunch as he placed the finished layout for the museum brochure on Amanda's desk.

She slid aside her tuna sandwich. "It's wonderful."

"As a team, *we're* wonderful."

Marco pulled up the chair and cracked open the soda can Amanda offered. "Did you know that Oakhurst Design Group has been approached about a hotel complex and retail center in Rehobeth?"

"On the beach?"

"So I heard."

Amanda narrowed her glance. "From whom did you hear?"

"The horse's mouth."

"You couldn't possibly mean Matthew Oakhurst, and I specifically asked you not to hang out with David until this campaign is over."

Marco looked properly disgusted. "Have I had a minute to hang out with anyone outside the office? Would I go against the hand that pays me?"

"You're leading up to something."

"Truth is, I ran into David last Saturday night. He's been running down to Rehobeth, trying to square the deal. Big stuff in the works."

"Last Saturday? You two were in some bar, I suppose."

"No, at the Grand Opera House. My date, Carla, had tickets to the symphony orchestra. We ran into David at intermission and got to talking business. There might be something in this for an aggressive ad agency."

"Yes, there might. Interesting. I'll make a note to check into it when we've finished up with this campaign." Amanda did her best to look disinterested.

Marco relaxed in his chair and smiled at her, his dark eyes sparkling. "It might mean you'd have to work with him again."

She perfected her nonchalance and answered as she finished her sandwich. "No conflict of interest in this one. Maybe I'll give the account to you. What did the orchestra play?"

"Haydn's Trumpet Concerto, some Mozart and Vivaldi."

"Lovely."

"Aren't you going to ask me who he was with?"

"No."

"A date. The man might have had a date."

"Marco, whom David keeps company with is none of my business."

He sipped from the can. "She was a perky little redhead. Patsy something."

"Thank you for that information." Amanda looked over the sketches. "Little and perky was never his type," she murmured to herself.

"Aha."

"Aha, nothing. David can date any type he wants to." She and Marco looked at each other.

"The answer to the question you can't bring yourself to ask is, yes, they seemed quite familiar with each other."

Amanda pointed resolutely at the door, and Marco left. A perky redhead. Well, why not? And good luck to her. David was a one-woman man, the one who had proposed too soon. Although their problems had been many, they had never been unfaithful.

During their marriage, she'd been out in the business world with single men every day. David's classes had been full of female students. The desire to make a clean break before either of them had found someone else was one of the things that had prompted the divorce, one of the things that had made it all seem so civilized. She doodled on the blotter with a felt-tipped pen.

In some ways it might have been better if he had come back to town with a wife and children. It would have forced a settling of the emotional upheaval much earlier.

When she finished the sandwich, she crossed the reception area to Marco's office. He was laying out another newspaper ad.

"Pull up a stool. I was expecting you."

"Why?"

Marco held the brush of rubber cement. "Because you want to know why I waited all week to tell you about running into David and Perky at the Opera House."

"No, I don't. I want to find out when the magazine layout for Cork World will be done."

"You took it in yesterday at lunch."

"So I did," Amanda said. "All right, you're dying to tell me why you waited. Spill it."

"Because Monday morning was too soon to get you all in a turmoil again. Believe it or not, boss, I prefer working for you when you're on an even keel. By the end of the week you seemed like your old self. Why rock the boat?"

"Marco, I don't appreciate your amateur psychology."

"Just simple observation. I get more accomplished when you're happy. Running into David doesn't seem to make you happy."

"I admit it was unsettling. You know perfectly well why I'm so concerned. This account is at stake."

"So you keep telling me. And yourself, I suspect."

"You know it's true. I saw him myself Friday night, and as you admit yourself, I've been fine. You're overreacting."

"No kidding, a date last Friday?"

"Of course not."

Marco slathered the page with glue. "You didn't tell me you saw him Friday, and I didn't tell you I saw him Saturday. It was worth waiting. I had a lot to do this week and so did you. At five o'clock I'll tell you the rest of it."

Amanda casually picked up a type-style book. "What rest of it?"

"You won't like it. I'll wait till work's finished."

She put her fingers around his wrist.

"Watch the glue, boss," Marco cried.

"What *rest of it?*"

"He and Perky are going to be at the Ad Council shindig tomorrow night."

"You're kidding."

Marco smiled paternalistically. "I do know a thing or two about women. Rule One, never tell them their ex-husbands will be at the same function until the last minute. It seems Perky works for the public-relations department of the PBS station in Philadelphia that covers Wilmington, too. She's taking David. Carla got all that out of her during intermission." Marco put the glue brush back into the bottle and tightened the cap. "Would you rather find yourself a bank president or somebody a little tonier to escort you?"

"Why?"

"Give David and Perky some competition in the date department. You know how those things work."

"D'Abruzzi, I have no interest in the *date department* and no intention of competing with anyone unless it's professional."

"I just want to make sure you enjoy yourself."

"As long as I'm on the other side of the ballroom, I'll enjoy myself. I'm taking you, and we're going to have a wonderful time, even if you have to dance."

"I like a woman with spunk."

On Saturday night David handed his car keys to the valet and offered his arm to Patsy Hornbach. He entered the Hotel DuPont, berating himself for ever having accepted her invitation to the Advertising Council evening. He'd accepted for one reason, and that reason was sure to leave him as strung out as he'd been a week earlier at the stables of River's Edge.

The crowd had already gathered. There were a dozen couples on the dance floor and others milling at the bar. David scanned it all as the two of them stood on the steps, then entered the Gold Ballroom. Patsy was already waving to fellow associates. "There's half a dozen people I want you to meet," she whispered.

"Don't worry about me."

She patted his arm. "Never." She smiled. "Nothing becomes a man more than a formal dinner jacket. You were obviously born in one."

Fraud crossed his mind. The beautiful woman on his arm considered him polished, to the manner born. She was entitled to whatever fantasy she had created for herself. He rarely discussed his background, or his aspirations for that matter. There had only been one woman in his life from whom he'd held nothing back. The one who'd first put him in a dinner jacket, the one who'd polished those rough edges. He glanced back at the entrance. The one who stood on the staircase at that moment with her arm through Marco D'Abruzzi's.

David stood stock-still and drank in the vision. The woman he'd last seen mucking out stalls now stood in low-heeled sandals. Her legs seemed endless. There was a sheen to her stockings, a silvery glimmer climbing up her calves to her knees where gossamer fluttered. Her dress—if that was what they called fabric that sheer— seemed to have no shape but hers.

There were thin straps at her shoulders, and that gossamer whatever-it-was clung here, fell there, over thighs, breasts, hips. A single strand of jade beads lay at her throat. She was a dozen shades of peach, ripe peach. His heartbeat increased to rib-cracking intensity.

She turned and greeted someone she obviously knew. David watched her laugh, watched her hair tumble as she nodded and shook hands. She and Marco chatted, then began to mingle. She moved with grace; she glowed. People approached her. There was another handshake, a quick buss on the cheek. She was in her element—and more than ever beyond his reach. Anxiety flickered through his desire as painful memories stirred.

"See someone you recognize?"

David nodded at Patsy's understatement. "The folks from Mendenhall and Lipton. They're bidding on our mill restoration."

"Of course. Marco was at the Opera House. Then this isn't a roomful of strangers."

For one long, aching moment he wished it were. He'd left the stables at River's Edge confident of his ability to maintain his equilibrium. He was quick with quips and fully aware of the power of surprise that continued to put her on the defensive. Amanda was incapable of hiding her emotions. It gave him the edge he'd established and maintained since the start. Since their first encounter, he'd welcomed her wrath, her frustration, her worry. As long as she was railing at him, it meant he had his own feelings well in hand.

He still had the element of surprise. He hadn't mentioned a thing about this evening to Marco. He'd have to move quickly, however, before Amanda or Marco realized he was there.

He turned to Patsy as he led her toward the staircase. "I suppose I ought to say hello." He maintained idle conversation as she walked with him through the sea of tuxedos and designer dresses.

He couldn't have orchestrated it better himself. Amanda's back was turned. Marco spotted them first and put out his hand to Patsy. "Look who's arrived," he said.

Amanda turned. She smiled first at Patsy, then glanced at him. There was color in her cheeks and her eyes shone. Something flashed in the velvety depths and disappeared. "David Smith," she said. "And you must be Patsy Hornbach. Marco said you two would be here. I understand you produce the public-service announcements for WPBS."

David stood through five minutes of animated conversation between Patsy and Amanda. Through it all his ex-wife neither looked at him nor acknowledged him again.

Ten

___

The periphery of the ballroom had been set with round linen-covered tables for eight, reflected in the tilted gilt mirrors that lined the room. By the time the employees of Mendenhall and Lipton, which also included Karen and her date, found their seats, Amanda had long finished her conversation with Patsy and David. Although she'd felt flushed throughout the entire conversation, nothing else hinted at her distress.

They ate a leisurely dinner, made idle conversation and then Marco turned to her. He tugged his lapel. "I can never keep these pleats flat. David Smith stops traffic in one of these things. His type was born in them."

Amanda shook her head. "His type has no more experience with them than your type."

"Come on. Your ex is no street kid from Boston's North End."

"You're the son of a stonemason in Boston. David's father is an electrician in Pittsburgh," she replied as she made a concerted effort not to scan the room for his table.

"Pittsburgh, as in steel mills and union wages?"

Amanda laughed. "Union wages."

Marco whispered. "You made a bigger mistake than I thought. A jazzy, rich girl like you *needs* a blue-collar boy. Gives you a better perspective on life."

"Marco, dear, I didn't invite you along tonight to discuss my perspective on life."

"Somebody has to."

"Not tonight. Tonight we discuss the advertising business."

Marco got to his feet. "Let's dance."

"All right," she replied as he rushed her onto the floor.

Once they'd settled among the other couples, Marco put his cheek next to hers. "Now, about the advertising business."

She pulled back and looked at him. "What are you up to?"

"That's *my* question."

"I don't know what you mean."

"We're *sympatico*. You're the best, Amanda, a top-notch administrator and account exec. I'm a damn good art director. I want a partnership. I want to invest financially in Mendenhall and Lipton, so we can expand." With a flourish he supported her back and lowered her into a dip. "But I need some assurance that you're not going to pack up and start again in Chicago or Des Moines."

Amanda clung to his shoulder. "What would ever make you think I'd leave Wilmington?"

"I'm Italian with three sisters. I know when a woman won't face her feelings. You put the entire United States between you and your architect the first time. I'm getting vibes, boss, vibrations telling me you think you need that kind of space again. You'd be a success anywhere in the country. Professionally it wouldn't hurt. Emotionally it won't solve a thing."

"You have no idea what you're talking about." The music stopped, and over the scattered applause Amanda finally looked into his sympathetic expression.

"Don't I? You're more confused than a kid in a candy shop. There's no place you can go to keep your emotions from catching up with you, not your house, the farm or Seattle." He tapped her temple. "Resolve it up here."

She moved his hand. "There is nothing to resolve."

"Yes, there is. Either you're still in love with David or you're not."

"I don't need this from you, Marco. Why can't you accept the fact that all of this has nothing to do with anything but business?"

"Because you can't. Why not just back out of the competition if you think your former relationship with David is in the way? Why not put your energy into something less migraine inspiring? We don't need the mill project."

"*I* need it."

"Not the way you thought you did. A month ago winning the Oakhurst account was for business. Now you need it as some proof for your ex-husband that you're good. He already knows that. You and I know it. Whatever this damn thing is with the two of you, finish it soon, *capeesh?*"

"It is finished. He's in love with a lovely woman, and I wish them well. He would say the same to me." She stopped at the sudden tap on her shoulder and turned to the intruder.

A dinner jacket did wonders for Marco D'Abruzzi, but it paled in comparison to what David Smith did for a dinner jacket.

David kept his hand on Amanda's shoulder long enough to feel her tremble. His own body betrayed him, however, as she glanced from his cummerbund, up along the pearl studs to his matching bow tie.

She glared. "David." A flush crept into her collarbone.

"Marco, I've come over here to persuade Dazzle to dance with me."

"She's all yours," Marco replied with a grin.

Amanda's deepening color reached her hint of cleavage. She put her hand to her throat. "I don't think so."

"For old times' sake. Just one."

"This is uncalled-for."

"It won't kill you."

"It might," Marco added as he moved away.

David settled her gently in his arms as the rustle of chiffon set his pulse pounding in half a dozen places. The respectful distance he kept between them teased until it became an ache he didn't dare savor. Had he expected this? Had he drummed up an excuse to speak with her just to hold her again? He began a decent box step. The slow music drew them into the dancers as they moved around the ballroom. He didn't need conversation. This was more than enough.

"Well?" she was saying.

"I'm sorry. What did you say?"

Under his open hand he felt Amanda arch her back. Her breasts brushed his chest as she looked at him. "I've done everything but beg you not to use that stupid nickname."

"I called you Dazzle again? I don't mean to. Old habits die hard. I never used your given name except when the justice of the peace asked me if I would take you, *Amanda*."

"You're trying my patience. We shouldn't be dancing."

He was close to agreeing with her for very different reasons. "It would seem more awkward if we didn't. Patsy wants me to mingle." He waited, sensing her curiosity. His equilibrium began to return as he danced.

"Have you been dating long?"

"A while." He ignored a stab of guilt. "Does that bother you?"

"Of course not. Your social life is none of my concern."

"Except when you're part of it."

"I'm not."

He smiled into her hair as she bristled. "Except tonight."

"This is business."

It didn't feel like business. He increased the pressure from his hand along her spine as he guided her over the floor. She arched again, and he felt as though he were easing down into a hot bath. Her breasts grazed his chest once, then again.

"We shouldn't be dancing like this." She was breathless.

"You're right."

"Well, then why...?" She looked up at him for the first time. His wide-open gaze held hers. "David, no," she whispered.

"No, what?"

She blinked. Confusion danced in her expression. "Nothing. Tell me about Patsy."

He looked briefly to the left. "She has lots of television types to talk business with. I think the way she put it was, 'Run Amanda around the dance floor while I drum up some accounts.' I must admit, you're looking positively sultry."

"Dancing with me was Patsy's idea?" A slow burn crept up over Amanda's collarbone again.

"Certainly."

"Nevertheless, if you're involved with someone, you had no business at my house, not to mention those other things. Have you told Patsy I'm your ex-wife?"

"She knows there's one out there somewhere. She had no idea it was you." He smiled. *This* he could savor. "You're old business, Amanda. That's all it was at your house. The kiss at the mill was an impetuous mistake, and I've apologized for what I said in your bedroom at the farm. You know why I was there."

"To see Scott."

"Who else?" Confusion again settled into her dark eyes, and he left her to her thoughts as they finished the fox trot.

His mistake was pulling her to him to avoid another couple. Their thighs brushed. His shirtfront and lapels continued to play a dangerous game with the sweep of chiffon over her breasts. All of it was deliciously familiar. Foolish, erotic memories lay so close to the surface that they simmered as he felt her breathing grow shallow.

He ached for her to admit to her own confusion. Surely she knew he could feel her denial. He could sense her doubts. Did she suspect that the unwarranted desire teasing her tore at him, as well?

Didn't she need to drop these foolish defenses? Didn't she long to confront what was so obvious? Couldn't she guess how he ached for a sign from her?

She brushed against him once more, and her breath caught as she stopped dancing. "I'd like to go back to my table if you don't mind."

At that moment Marco came into sight. He was with Patsy, heading for them as the music died. "Look who I found," the art director said cheerfully when the four of them stood together.

Patsy smiled at Amanda. "WPBS will be doing a documentary on the mill restoration once they break ground. If you get the account, I'd love to run my ideas past you. I've learned from experience that if a public-relations firm is involved, projects tend to run smoother. It makes communication much easier."

"I look forward to it," Amanda replied without looking at David.

"Okay, Hot Stuff, it's our turn again. Don't even think about turning me down. I'm in this monkey suit for you."

The couples parted as the orchestra resumed playing. Over Patsy's curls David watched as Marco took Amanda into his arms, and she moved gracefully to the music. It had been a long time since social situations produced extremes in his respiratory system. He damned his inability to control his reactions and the settling sadness that tightened his chest.

David awoke to an empty September Sunday, much of it already slept away. The night had dragged on relentlessly, ending far differently than he had imagined. He blinked and buried his head in his pillow, disoriented by the unfamiliar surroundings.

It took a shower to clear his head of the conversation fragments still bouncing around his skull, and a cup of coffee to make sense of his response. He poured a second cup and ambled out onto the lawn bordering the bridle path that joined the estates. As he reviewed the night, Jace Lydon came down the hill with a section of the Sunday paper.

"Have you seen the society pages yet?"

"I haven't even bought a paper."

Jace handed him a section. "Mom was reading it over lunch. She thought you might be interested in a few of the photos."

David reached for his glasses and scanned the newsprint. There was a full two-page spread of informal photographs around the headline Annual Ad Council Ball Was the Place to Be. The sea of unfamiliar faces in casual poses blurred until one nearly jumped off the page at him. He looked at Jace and swore.

In glorious black and white Amanda was gazing at him like a lost lamb. He was smiling at her. They were in each other's arms, looking as though they belonged together. He read the caption beneath the photograph: "While waltzing, Amanda Mendenhall, president of Mendenhall and Lipton, and her ex-husband, Philadelphia architect David Smith, discuss plans for a Chadds Ford mill restoration he's designed for his firm, Oakhurst Design Group."

Eleven

"It was a fox trot," Amanda muttered twenty minutes later in her Wilmington town house. She yanked up the paper, read it again and put it down. "Fifteen minutes out of the whole night, fifteen minutes. Why," she moaned, "did I ever dance with him? Idiot! Why did he ask me?"

Amanda paced across the room and stopped, finally, at the mantelpiece. Her open hand was cold and trembling in contrast to the heat of her cheek. She blinked, but it did no good. Tears filled her eyes; she wiped them furiously with a swipe of her sleeve. She wasn't about to cry.

She needed to go to the source of her misery, even if it took an hour's worth of detective work to find him. David had said he lived in Philadelphia, but that could mean any number of places from Center City to one of the suburbs. Maybe he'd already moved to the carriage house. Maybe he was at Patsy's. She pulled out her metropolitan phone book. D. Smith and David Smith filled half a column. She tried Marco, then her brother. There was no answer at either place. She hung up, paced again and went to her desk in the kitchen.

She pressed her hands against the countertop. Slivers of pain were already shooting behind her eyes. She hated what she knew she had to do, but putting it off only increased the tension.

No doubt the morning after a formal, romantic evening would find David with the perky redhead, probably having brunch and a good laugh over the society page of the paper. Amanda flipped the pages of the phone book. There were three Hornbachs. One P. Hornbach was listed on Delancy Place, a Society Hill street in Philadelphia. Amanda lifted the receiver, watched her hand tremble, inhaled and tapped out the number. A female voice answered.

"Patsy?"

"Yes?"

Amanda's throat ached as she introduced herself. "I'm terribly sorry to bother you, but I need to get in touch with David about business. I thought he might be with you."

"With me?"

"Or you could give me his phone number. I'm afraid I don't know how to find him."

"He's been living on Spruce Street, but he moved out to a carriage house in Chadds Ford, the Lydons'. Sycamore Hill. The phone hookup is tomorrow afternoon," she replied. There was the briefest hesitation. "As far as I know, he's there. I haven't seen him since last night."

"Thank you," Amanda managed as she placed the receiver back in its cradle. No phone. Probably hadn't seen the paper, wouldn't care if he had. Sweet oblivion.

In a vain attempt to keep the tension under control she pulled on khaki shorts and a loose T-shirt and scrubbed the kitchen counters. Over the antiseptic smell of household cleaner she imagined herself facing Leo and Ira Brachman. Would contractors care? Would the Conservation Council voice its concern? Would Matthew Oakhurst demand an explanation? They all thought Mendenhall and Lipton was small potatoes in the advertising world. Why hadn't she mentioned her marriage the moment David had waltzed into the boardroom that fateful April afternoon?

There was no choice but to sit down with each party involved in the account. She would explain as a businesswoman, one-on-one. There was nothing else to do but approach it as a man would. She had a problem. She'd see that everything was explained. She'd make sure she understood their feelings and they understood the situation, then be done with it. Nothing else would do.

The closest parking spot was half a block from the row house, and David muttered to himself all the way from his car to the polished brass knocker on Amanda's front door. He had on old jeans, a cotton crewneck sweater and an anxious expression. What was it about the woman that garnered his sympathy, that found him wanting to waste a perfectly beautiful Sunday afternoon facing her wrath?

He knocked. The door opened. Amanda stood before him in dirty shorts and a smudged shirt. "David!"

"I saw the paper. I moved Saturday, and there's no phone yet."

"You could have used the Lydons'." She started to close the door.

"Amanda, give me some credit! I drove all the way down here to hash this out."

"Not to apologize?"

"I don't recall you kicking and screaming in protest as I asked you to dance."

"I should have."

"You didn't. Stop looking at me as though someone's put ice down your back."

She brushed at dirt on the hem of her shorts. "You're always popping up where you don't belong. I never expected you. You shouldn't have come."

"Amanda, you have enough decisions to make in your own life. Let me decide what I should and shouldn't do in mine. I thought you might like to take a walk and talk this out. It's still warm and gorgeous out here. I'll bet you've been holed up in there since you bought the stupid paper."

"I don't feel like walking. I've been cleaning the kitchen." She pressed two fingers against her temple.

"A good, healthy way to work off some tension? Hasn't helped the headache, I guess." He climbed the steps and pushed her gently inside with him. "If you don't want to walk, then we'll stand in the living room or sit on the couch. Very flattering shot of us at least."

"How can you joke?"

"The damage is done," he replied quietly. "I was just trying to be positive."

Amanda stood with him in the living room. "Positive! We're on the society page, complete with caption that we were married."

"We *were* married."

"I should have known you'd make a joke of it. This isn't funny. This was my biggest fear. It will all be misconstrued. I never should have danced with you. Never. The picture makes us look like we were enjoying ourselves."

He laughed. "Heaven forbid."

"You know what I mean. This photo gives an erroneous impression. You know what the Brachmans will think! You know how reluctant Wilkins is to give me the account. All they need is to see that stupid photo, which makes it look as though we're honeymooning. I can't remember so much as smiling at you last night. Where on earth was the photographer?"

"Damned if I know. I never saw one, let alone somebody jotting down copy. You must admit, it makes a good story."

"It's cheap sensationalism. We never lived here when we were married. We only came down for holidays. It was over when I left New York for Seattle, and it has nothing to do with Wilmington's advertising business."

"It does look as though we were enjoying ourselves." He looked at her. "I'm sorry you're so upset, but I've said all along that your fears are groundless. It's part of our past, that's all."

"Do you honestly believe that?" She faltered. "Please, I need your opinion." Amanda stopped and pressed her fingers against her forehead. "You know the men involved in the project. You know how they think. Will they see this as collusion? Could it jeopardize anything when federal grants and government subsidies are involved?''

"I don't know," David replied quietly. "I think the men heading up this project will want an explanation, that's all."

Lipton rubbed himself against Amanda's ankles. She picked him up and sighed.

"Maybe it was a mistake to drive all the way down here. You should be alone with your misery." He walked across the room and got as far as the door.

"David?"

Her plea registered in his chest. "What?"

"I need you to help me sort this out. I don't have anyone else."

"No Marco to the rescue?"

"This is between you and me."

He came back to her. "Then you and I will solve it."

Amanda closed her eyes and inhaled. "As I see it, I'll have to take tomorrow morning and chase down everybody to explain why I didn't say anything in the first place. I'd like you to be with me. Then I want you to remove yourself from the judging of my presentation as well as the other agencies'. If your associates don't already know, tell them about Patsy. The fact that you're in love with someone else can only help."

"Patsy? Don't muddy this up with another woman."

"But the fact that you're involved—"

He stared at her as he had the night before, a hundred times, a thousand. Now, as then, every fiber in him stirred. He put out his hand, then slowly withdrew it. "I won't sit on the panel. You're right about that. But I'm not about to bring my personal life into this any more than I have to."

She fought for composure. "You're in love with someone else. Can't you see the difference that could make?"

His chest tightened, but all he said was "Amanda, another woman won't be a factor. I'm not going to turn this into a soap opera to land a business account for you."

"Is that how it looks to you?" Her voice broke and she turned away. "I don't want to use anyone. I just need your help."

Without thinking he put his hand out again.

"Damn it, I need you tomorrow," she whispered. Tears already hung in her lashes. "Please go," she choked as she opened her hands over her face and pressed her eyes.

He didn't go. For a fraction of a moment he marveled at this side of her, a side she'd never exposed, never possessed, for all he'd known. He wrapped his arms around her and stood as she stayed rigid. The feel of her nearly undid him as she cringed at first and cried into her fingers, with her elbows and forearms pressed against his chest. He offered strength while she was at her weakest, and gradually five feet nine inches of woman moved against him. He opened his hand against the crown of her head as she held on, her arms finally around his neck.

Instinctively he pressed his free hand against the small of her back. "Let go," he whispered at her temple. "For once in your life, just let go."

"I'm sorry," she choked.

With every ounce of self-control he possessed David stood rock still with her. "It's all right. I'm not going to talk. No teasing, no lecture."

Relief seemed to push her anguish over the edge. She cried until there was nothing left and burrowed against his immovable strength. As the storm in her abated, his own turmoil increased. Reason flickered in her expression as she gasped gently for air and he kissed her forehead. She looked up at him, and before he could stop himself he kissed her mouth.

Her lips were warm, parted. He felt her shudder as she responded. Then, just as quickly, she shook her head. "This can't be."

Grief tore at him. He was the first to loosen the hug. He moved his fingers through her hair and pushed away loose strands caught against her damp cheek. "You were never much of a crier," he murmured, "but, oh, you could kiss, Dazzle. Are you sure these tears were all over business?"

Amanda tried to look away, still hiccuping as calm returned. "Of course. Please forgive me and forget about it. The tears and the kiss were completely uncalled-for."

David cupped her face and forced her to look at him. "I'd say both were long overdue. You've been a wound-up spring since I jumped at you on the sidewalk two weeks ago. Let's hope this has done you some good."

"It's the stress of the account. I can't afford any problems. I'm the least likely candidate for the account to begin with and now this."

David kept his hands on her face. "Is it the account?"

"Yes. My lack of composure is humiliating."

David put his hand on the back of her head again and pressed her face against his shoulder. "I don't remember your ever saying you needed me, Amanda, not until today." His voice was low, soothing. Slowly she raised her arms from her sides and lightly wrapped them around him. He felt her spine beneath the shirt. She was quiet, but as a final tremor made her shiver, he tensed. She took a long, deep breath before she stepped back. This time he let her go reluctantly.

"What I need is your help, David."

"It must tear your heart out to ask. It always did."

"I'm not begging, and I'll regret till I die that I fell apart just now."

"Good blackmail material. You've let your exhusband see that you're not invincible. There goes the agency down the tubes."

"This is hardly the time for jokes."

"Want to cry some more? I can hug you again." He started toward her, and she pushed him away.

"You're impossible. I wish you'd go."

"No, you don't, not yet. As you see it, I've helped put you in this mess and I'm the one to help get you out. Your head must be splitting over this one. Shall I make some tea while you get the aspirin?"

"I can take care of that myself. I really do think you should go."

David looped a hank of hair behind her ear. "I didn't ask if you could take care of it yourself. I asked if you'd like me to do it."

"No, thank you. You know what I'd like you to do. I'll be at your office by eight tomorrow morning, and I assure you, I'll be fine by then."

"You're pretending to be fine now."

"This isn't pretense. You shouldn't be here. I'll see you at your office." She started toward the door.

When he was back out on the stoop, he turned on the bottom step and looked up at her. "It's not too late for a walk. How about it?"

"I don't think so."

"Amanda, look at me." He watched her blink, her lashes still damp triangles. "Back then, in those crazy days, did you ever need me?"

She paused. "It was a long time ago. What good would it have done to need you? You didn't have time for me. You barely had enough time for your own needs."

Twelve

At seven-fifteen Monday morning Marco called Amanda. "Shove some bread in the toaster. I'm coming over for breakfast."

"Not this morning. I'm meeting David at his office."

"I saw the paper yesterday. That's why I'm calling. It's resolved. That's why I'm coming over." He hung up before she could get anything more from him. In the twenty minutes it took for Marco to arrive she paced, swore out loud to Lipton and fought her curiosity.

The moment Marco bounded up her front steps she opened the door. "Good morning," he said. "Toast ready?"

"Start talking," she replied as she followed him through the house.

Marco picked up the cat. "What a day. Must be seventy degrees again. Gonna be a beautiful week to wrap this up, Dazzle. I see you're dressed for success.''

She scoffed. Unlike Marco's artistic attire of pleated maroon plants, Italian moccasins and loose, drop-shouldered shirt, she had on a linen jacket and skirt, with a silk print scarf artistically draped and pinned over one shoulder. Her hair was held back with combs over each ear. ''It's important that I look serious.''

Marco pushed down the toaster slide. ''We all know you're serious. May I call you Dazzle? I really like it.''

''No.''

''Not serious enough?''

''Marco, you had better start explaining. I'm supposed to go to the Oakhurst office this morning.''

''Butter my toast and I will. David called me this morning at six-thirty from a pay phone, no less. What an ungodly hour. His message is this. Yesterday after he left here he got in touch with everybody you're worried about. He wants you to know he saw each of them personally—no phone calls.''

''Oh, Marco,'' she said quietly.

The art director smiled. ''He wants to make sure that I make you understand that what needed to be said has been said, man-to-man. Don't foul it up by running around and talking to these guys all over again. David said the problem of your marriage has been discussed and dismissed. Don't stir up waters that have settled. Those were his words.''

''Don't foul things up? Does he think I'm helpless? He wasn't to do this all himself. Man-to-man. I hate that expression.''

''Apparently he thought it was necessary. He handled it the way he knew would work to our advantage.''

"He should have told me what he was going to do."

Marco took the toast. "Amanda, this is a gift horse I'm talking about. Don't look it in the mouth. You asked for his help, and he gave it to you. The guy was there when you needed him. Enough already!"

She glared. "Why did he tell you all this and not me?"

Her associate ate his toast.

"You're hedging, D'Abruzzi."

"I'm chewing."

"Well, swallow."

Marco was thoughtful. "What he said and what he meant might not be the same thing. He told me it's a clean break. He's messed things up, and now he's set them straight. That's what you wanted. He said you don't need any more pressure this week, as in the pressure of having to deal with him. This way you don't have to see him."

"Why wouldn't he mean that?" she asked.

"Because if you'd stop thinking only about yourself for ten minutes, you might see that *he* doesn't need any more pressure, either." Marco polished off the last of his toast.

"The pressure of dealing with me."

"Yes." And then, more kindly, Marco added, "Whichever way he meant it, you and I can finish this presentation. Want to tell me what happened here yesterday?"

"No. That is, nothing happened. He simply came over, and we talked about the problem."

"The business problem or the being-in-love-with-him problem?"

Amanda scowled and fought the guilt settling on her. "Don't be ludicrous. He's in love with Perky Patsy."

"Love presents a problem."

"You're as impossible as he is."

"You're complicating his life, boss. Keep in mind that Friday it'll all be over. Isn't that what you want to believe? Stop worrying, and tell me again how you won't pull up stakes and open an agency west of the Mississippi. Got any coffee?"

Marco and Amanda entered Mendenhall and Lipton together. Karen came from behind her desk and followed them. "You think you know a person when she's your boss."

Amanda smiled. "You know me quite well, Karen."

"Hah! I had to read in the paper just who David Smith is, or should I say was?"

"Whom."

"You know very well whom. Why didn't you tell me you were married to him? And what ever possessed you to give him up?"

"David and I are history. We were young, headstrong and very mistaken."

Karen sighed. "Do you think he's serious about that redhead from the PBS station?"

Marco took her by the hand and headed for his office. "Let's talk business. For starters, I need four pages of clean copy typed."

"I don't want to talk business, Marco. I want to talk about David. Amanda doesn't want him. What's the big deal?"

Marco closed his office door before Amanda could hear his reply. She went into her own office and sat at her desk. How simplistic to say she didn't want him. Karen was twenty-two, the age at which Amanda had thought David was all she wanted, all she'd ever need.

Need. What a simplistic word for such a heartrending emotion.

Never before or since had she failed anyone as she'd failed David Smith. Even now she continued to misread him. It still embarrassed her to think how she'd misinterpreted his actions in the past two weeks. Marco was right. She never gave his own confusion a thought. It was obvious that he was after assurances that what had passed as love between them was gone, maybe had never been there to begin with. He was in love with someone new.

Her teary outburst had been cathartic. Tears in private would have been less embarrassing. Nevertheless, Amanda felt renewed. The tears and David's chivalry had closed a chapter. As angry as she was that he'd gone to the Brachmans and the others without her, she felt better than she had in days, maybe even grateful for his resolutions. She was ready to get the Oakhurst account squared away, ready to turn the page on her life. She got back to work.

Tuesday and Wednesday it rained, light showers that gave way to clear skies on Thursday. Potted mums were beginning to appear in window boxes, the Rodney Square foliage was darkening. When the rain stopped, the temperature cooled, giving everyone a dose of the autumn to come.

She ate a bag lunch in the square with Karen on Thursday, and neither mentioned the architect by name. It felt like old times. By Thursday afternoon Marco and Amanda had the presentation as polished as it would ever be. The dummy brochure was clean, the storyboards complete. Amanda reviewed her financial figures, her estimates for printing costs, numbers for the runs and suggestions for an expanded public-relations program. She had the entire package photocopied, one for each of the men she knew would be present at Friday's meeting.

The week went so fast that Amanda had little time to concentrate on anything but business. There was enough homework to keep her at her computer screen till well past the thinking hours, and enough excitement over Friday morning to keep her mind on track.

When the day finally arrived, it was glorious. She dressed well in low-heeled, fine kid pumps. Her height, and a well-cut teal suit, understated her curvaceous figure. Full breasts and a slim waist might sell everything from cars to toothpaste, but in the male-oriented business end of advertising, there was no advantage to flaunting one's womanliness.

Her appointment at the Conservation Council office was scheduled for 10:00 a.m. At nine-thirty Marco helped her pack up her briefcase and portfolio.

Amanda smiled and grabbed his hand. "Wish me luck."

"Icy!" He rubbed her fingers. "You'll be wonderful. Most of it's my brilliant artwork and design, anyway."

Although David had removed himself from the selection, Matt Oakhurst had insisted that he still attend each presentation. On Friday he arrived dutifully at the Tenth Street offices as the others were gathering.

They met again in the conference room: Leo and Ira Brachman, sixtyish contractors, all nuts and bolts; John Wilkins, early forties, stiff, intellectual, the environmental activist; Matthew Oakhurst, a short man with an enormous talent and reputation, head of the firm David took such pride in belonging to.

Amanda entered as they were taking their seats, and they all got back onto their feet. She smiled. Lord how she lit up a room. There were handshakes, small talk and then the four other men were suddenly quiet. He fought a flush as they looked from him back to her. Distress flickered in her expression, but she offered her hand.

"David."

He took it. "Amanda."

She looked at the assembled group. "David tells me that he's explained about our brief relationship, the photograph and the other evening. He assures me that you understand that I had no idea he was employed in this area, and that I have had no contact with him for the past six years."

David put on his reading glasses and cleared his throat, hoping she'd realize there was no point in grinding him into the dust.

John Wilkins called them to order. "We're anxious to see what you've brought, Amanda. In deference to your previous relationship, David won't be offering an opinion on this or any of the other agency presentations. There's much at stake in this project, and he's wise not to jeopardize it."

David winced at the wrist slapping.

"I'm anxious to hear what you can do for us, Amanda," Matt added.

David caught the relief in her expression. She smiled again and began her presentation in the low, throaty voice that had always mesmerized him. For an hour she explained what Mendenhall and Lipton proposed to do for the future museum.

Each of the men looked carefully at the artwork and accompanying copy. Each was sincere in his praise. It was David who added that she was the first of the three agencies bidding. John Wilkins said they intended to make a decision by midweek. There was another round of handshakes, thanks, and then she was gone, back out into the spring afternoon.

By the time David got to a phone an hour later, there was nothing but a taped message at her office. Mendenhall and Lipton had finished for the week.

Thirteen

—

River's Edge on a fall afternoon was as close to heaven as Amanda expected to get for a while and better than a tranquilizer for unknotting tension. Late Friday the house was quiet, but well tended as always. Hannah had left sweet rolls in the pantry and fresh towels upstairs in the bathroom. Hank had begun planting spring bulbs in the beds around the porch. Amanda dropped her weekend bag and opened her window.

The day had grown uncommonly warm, an Indian-summer, daydreaming, puppy-love afternoon. Her mood was bright, and for the first time in weeks she relaxed. The temperature was bound to drop, her mood was bound to sag, but for now she had nothing on her mind but taking advantage of the tranquillity. The estate and the afternoon were hers.

Instead of a bra she pulled on a faded top from an old bikini under a loose pullover shirt, boxer-style tennis shorts and good white sneakers. The backboard on the family tennis court was always ready.

She followed Lipton down the hill to the court. It sat, with the swimming pool, on the east side of the house, secluded by generations of mature rhododendrons and boxwood. Both had been designed to take advantage of the outbuilding that had originally been an ice-house. Her father had turned it into a clubhouse, tearing out one side of the stuccoed fieldstone and adding plumbing, dressing rooms, a small kitchenette and seating area, all of which opened onto a brick patio.

The building still held remnants of summer activities. Pool goggles and kickboards of her nieces and nephews lay on the shelves. Pads were still on the chaise longues, and the sailcloth curtains partitioning the dressing areas were due for the fall cleaning. Amanda found her tennis racket and a can of balls and went back outside to the backboard.

The three o'clock sun warmed her legs and shoulders as she played. The rhythmic thwack, thwack, thwack as the ball hit the board did as much for her tension as Sunday's tears. An occasional car out on the road and the sound of the ball were all that disturbed the sweet air.

As she hit the ball with her steady swing, she tried to review her presentation. She attempted to recall the figures, Marco's designs and the men considering them, but David's image was a constant interruption. The memory of him as he sat, glasses in hand, listening attentively, ruined her concentration.

Even alone on the tennis court embarrassment quickened her pulse as she thought about Sunday's emotional collapse. She had no business being in his arms, not for any reason.

"Amanda?"

The sound of her name made her stop and turn, but there was no one in sight. She stooped for the ball and twirled her racket.

"Scott?" she called back toward the rhododen-drons.

In reply David rounded the boxwood.

"This is a surprise." She pushed her hair off the back of her neck to hide the perpetual jolt to her respiratory system. She felt him watch as she walked to the edge of the court and picked up the can of balls.

"I thought you deserved some congratulating. I stopped by your office, tried your house. This was on my way home. I'm just over the hill now, you know."

She nodded. "I know. It isn't even four o'clock. Are you playing hooky?"

Although he still had on his pleated pants, the tie was gone and his shirtsleeves were rolled up to his elbows. There were traces of mud on his boat shoes. "I had to check the mill site, last stop of the day. After all the trauma you've been through, I wanted to tell you myself that you did a great job today."

"Thank you." The air hummed with their silence, and Amanda's scalp tingled as she tried to put her thoughts together. "David," she said at last, "I'm sorry about my behavior last Sunday. I don't usually...everything had piled up. I behaved very unwisely. We never should have...you shouldn't have come to the house."

"Will you ever stop telling me what I should and shouldn't do?"

"In this case it's justified." She watched the breeze in the pine tops. "I didn't mean for you to speak to everyone without me. You didn't need to take over as if I were totally helpless.''

"No one would ever mistake you for helpless. I know the men involved far better than you do. I used my judgment. I did what I thought was best. Is it so hard just to say thank you?''

"Thank you.''

"Those two words never did come easily from you.''

"What do you expect? If you hadn't danced with me, there wouldn't have been any problem in the first place.''

He shrugged. "And if I hadn't designed the mill for Oakhurst or you were still in Seattle, none of this would have happened, either. In fact, if I'd gotten a scholarship to Cornell instead of Penn, we never would have met. If we'd never met, we'd never have married. How far back should I go?''

"Stop hiding behind sarcasm.''

"Darling Amanda, I'm not the one who's hiding. You can't accept honest emotion even when it smothers you.''

"I can accept blame when I deserve it. You shouldn't have come near me Saturday night.''

"We've had this discussion. I don't recall dragging you onto the dance floor. Life is what you've made it.''

"For the past six years I've been making it just fine.''

"And now, suddenly, you're confused about all of this. Worse still, you're obligated because I rescued the situation on my own, the way I thought was right.''

Amanda looked at him, at the blue eyes and his expectant expression. "I didn't need that much rescuing.''

"Sunday afternoon that's exactly what you needed.''

"I've apologized for that."

"It isn't necessary, Amanda. Much as you hate to think about it, you needed me and I came through."

"The way I never did for you?"

"Was that what you thought I'd say next? What good is it doing either of us to play every conversation off bitter memories of what we did or didn't do years ago?"

"No good. None of this is any good." From where they stood on the rise Amanda could see his Jeep at the stable courtyard. She put her racket on the patio table and began to walk. David simply matched her stride. The emotional turmoil continued to churn. Her guilt over being in his arms Sunday increased the memory of the episode. She stepped sideways to widen the distance between them.

"What did you say to the men?" she asked finally as they reached the courtyard.

"Only what the men needed to know."

"I hope you explained that it's completely over. Did you tell them about Patsy?"

As they reached the Jeep, David leaned back against the door and looked at the stables. "Patsy and I have made some decisions. She knows me well, better than I know myself. Perceptive as they come. She was the first to point out what's been increasingly obvious."

Under the cotton of her shirt Amanda's chest expanded against the binding of her old bikini top. She braced herself for his engagement announcement.

"Patsy and I have called it quits. It was as painless as these things go, mutual, no hard feelings."

Amanda's heart jumped in confusion. "I don't understand."

"Dazzle, darling, I think you do."

* * *

David watched as she stared across the cobblestones to a hay bale. "I'm sorry, truly."

In response he put his hands on her shoulders and leaned her against the car. "Don't be. There are too many questions here." The warmth of the sun seeped into his spine and the heat under his fingers radiated. He kissed her, his mouth soft against hers, gentle at first. She moaned softly. He strained against her, a waltz to their own music. Physical desire as strong as the days when they thought they'd die without each other swept over him. He hadn't even parted his lips.

As suddenly as he'd crushed her against him, he stood back. When he could speak, he smiled at her gasping and looked directly into her troubled expression. "It's still there."

"I think you should go," she managed.

"Tell me that's what you want."

She held her breath. "That's what I want." Sharply Amanda moved her trembling fingers in a wave and turned on her heels. She headed back for the tennis courts without looking back.

Did she have a clue as to what she wanted? Did she mean for him to leave, or did she expect him to follow, to catch up, to grab her and crush her to him? He was finished with being rejected, with guessing games. He watched her walk away, savoring the familiarity of her gait. Let her simmer.

When the massive thumping in his chest slowed, he started his car and drove around the bend to the Lydons' carriage house. Twenty minutes later he walked back, taking the bridle path from Sycamore Hill to the Mendenhall tennis court. He could hear the rhythmic

thwack of the ball hitting the backboard. He imagined
Amanda cursing him with each swing.

Apprehension and expectation tightened his muscles. The hammering in his chest increased as she
caught sight of him and missed her shot. He walked
across the lawn as he'd marched down Market Street,
emotion playing openly over his high cheekbones. This
time he was carrying a bottle of champagne and two
tulip-shaped glasses.

"Is your tennis as good as ever?"

"About as good as your continuing ability to startle
the daylights out of me. I thought you went home."
She looked at the bottle.

"Home doesn't settle anything. Tell me about your
game."

"What?"

"Tennis. You and I are going to start with conversation, the stuff we never had the first time around."

Her sigh was enormous. "David, please. I'm so
confused."

"That makes two of us."

"Perverse," she muttered, but she smiled. "My
tennis is so-so. I need to play regularly."

"I interrupted."

"Yes," she replied. "I wish tennis were all you've
interrupted."

"Amanda, it's important that I tell you what I
thought of your work this morning. I never saw much
from the inside last time around when we were married. I never took the time."

"You never had the time."

He uncorked the bottle and filled their glasses. "This
is for you, for all the times I didn't say congratula-
tions."

Her expression softened. "I don't know what to say."

"Of course you do."

"Thank you, David."

"You're welcome, Amanda." They sipped in silence, not completely comfortable. "Was that it, we never had time? I look at you now, and nothing's clear."

"What's the point in rehashing this? It's over."

"You can't look at me and say that. You may not know any more than I do about what's going on, but you feel it. God, you feel it, too. Have you been so preoccupied with your own misery that it's never occurred to you that I have my own? Your confusion tortures me."

"And you can't see how hard I've tried to avoid that? Stay away from me, David!"

"I can't! In one afternoon you turned my life upside down. I've been selfish, arrogant, aggressive because I have to make peace with this gut-wrenching need that's tearing me apart."

"You've made it artistically and financially. You have your career, your friends, the woman you love. Your life's in order."

"My life's in chaos because of the woman *I loved*. There's no place for any other woman in my life until I make sense of what's still between us."

"I think it's safer if we walk," she whispered. Empty glasses in hand, she started across the lawn again. He followed.

David glanced sideways at her. "You've been dead to me for six years. I hadn't seen you, hadn't thought about you. For six years I've gone on, worked out my problems, smoothed out my life, then bam! You're back."

"This chemistry business, these sparks won't last. They didn't the last time. I hope at least we've learned from our mistake."

"Amanda, I'm not the person I was then. You aren't, either. Even when you try not to look at me I can see how much you feel, how strongly you react. The brick wall's falling over on you, too, and here you stand, trying to push it back with your two little hands." He didn't dare touch her again. September and champagne had pulled the plug on his common sense. When she didn't answer, he didn't persist. They walked.

She held the empty glasses up and watched the late sunlight refract in the crystal. He watched as she made rainbows play on his chest. He felt the breeze move through his hair and flutter his collar. She glanced at his watchband and the buckle of his belt, his shoes.

"I've been afraid to look at you," she whispered.

"Do you know how you feel against me? Sunday, when you cried, I could have stood there holding you all afternoon. That's when I knew there's no chance of moving forward till I resolve what I left behind." He stopped as they reached the courtyard. "I was proud of you this morning. You handled everything so professionally."

"I've had a lot of practice. This is my work. I'm good at it."

"I knew you would be. I should have told you back . . . before."

"I wish you had."

"I couldn't. The better you were at your job, the less you needed us."

"Independence has its advantages," she said.

"Damn independence."

They looked at each other. The champagne had warmed him and obviously calmed Amanda's bout of nerves. She stood before him, one sultry, talented, sensuous unanswered question. "I don't want to feel this way."

"No one has to know, Dazzle. No one but the two of us."

"You have so much talent, David. I'm glad you're doing what you've always wanted. New York nearly snuffed that out."

"I was never big on patience. Oakhurst is exactly what I've wanted."

"Then let this be a truce. Wilmington has to be big enough for both of us."

The horses were out to pasture with the weather so warm, and the clean stalls smelled of fresh hay. Amanda and David resumed their stroll, the pauses between them easy but expectant. At the open arch to the empty stable she stopped.

"You're thinking that if we walk in there," he said, "I'll remember that Fourth of July. I think it was that stall on the right."

"It was," she whispered.

He pointed ahead. "There was no stopping you."

The champagne and sun made her flush as the reverie fluttered her nerves. David took the glasses from her and put his hands at her temples. "Maybe if we step back away from each other, we'll get close enough to remember why it didn't work. Right now I'll be damned if I know. I watched you this morning, and all I could remember was the robe, the way you move in that satin, the way you felt against me on Sunday. All of it felt good. Everything now feels even better. What went wrong, Dazzle?'' He pushed his fingers through her hair, and she tilted her head before she meant to.

The kiss was full of desperation and denial as she let him part her lips with his tongue. He kissed her hair. ''No one else feels like you.''

It was all so deliciously familiar. She held his face and showered his mouth with kisses as the memory of David, hungry, passionate, playful, took her back to the fresh hay and the empty stall on that Fourth of July. She'd laughed at her handsome husband as he'd pulled off their clothes. Moments later she'd cried for him until he'd covered her mouth with his to keep them from being discovered. Now, in this other life, desire tore through her as she tried to push the reverie away.

''I remember it, too,'' David said at her ear. ''I've done nothing these past weeks but remember.''

She broke away and looked at him. He was still handsome, determined, passionate. He'd added distance in the past few years. They both had. Had she ever known him? Had she ever taken the time? When she began to walk back toward the courts, he followed.

They reached the clubhouse together, and again he kissed her. ''I want another beginning, one with our eyes open. I brought more than champagne out here this afternoon, Amanda. I brought days' and days', maybe six years' worth of questions.'' He put his hand into his pocket and pulled out a foil packet. ''I've even got protection. Make love to me. Let me make love to you. It was always the one way we could communicate. Lie with me, talk, tell me, for once, what it is you want. I need answers.''

"I don't know," she cried, but she did know. Every fiber in her body had been awakened by her need for him. She was alive with it, like spring itself. "Making love to you would compromise everything you told the Brachmans. It makes it all a lie. The Conservation Council—"

He kissed the words away and put his hands over her breasts. "You've made your presentation."

"But I'll win the account. I'll be working with you."

"Then make a choice. Now, here." He kissed her neck and caressed her hips. "Stop me."

"So you'll have proof that my work is more important than making love to you?" She leaned into him and arched her back. "Don't make this a contest over control."

David's glance, already dusky with desire, darkened. He opened his hands in her hair. "We can make sense of this later."

She was a woman alive, and her body welcomed his touch, responding instantly to every sigh. Her growing desperation to be swept away made her voice raspy and soft. Her breathing was shallow, the color already high in her cheeks. "We can't. I won't. For your sake."

"Amanda!"

"Clear your head, David. You need rescuing from your own emotions. This isn't about control. I'm not out to prove that my work is more important. Making love to me compromises *you*. I'm only an account executive vying for Oakhurst's approval, but you're their rising star. You have a career with Matthew Oakhurst, one that won't be helped if he—or any of the others— think you weren't completely honest about our relationship. If any of them thought for one minute that you seduced me... You are, you know. Seducing me."

He nuzzled her neck. "It's something we were both very good at. Come into the clubhouse before your reasoning begins to make sense to me."

"I have half a mind to follow you just to get this whatever-it-is between us out of my system."

"And once would do it?"

"Neither of us is in a position to find out."

He kissed her again. "You're right. Prone is the position for finding out."

"David." She stepped away and stood in front of him, panting softly. "I won't let you jeopardize your talent and your reputation over something as trivial as hormones."

"Trust me on this one. There's nothing trivial about my hormones."

Amanda put her fingers to his cheeks. "You're a very persuasive man."

"Not persuasive enough, however."

"There's enough we need to forgive each other for. Ruining your future and our reputations with Matthew Oakhurst can't be two things more. I want you to go. You need to leave. Now, before we make another mistake."

He covered her fingers with his hand. "The hell of it is, I know you're right."

"Then please go back to the Lydons'."

"I need the distance of another planet." He kissed her hard on the mouth. "There'll be a right time. I swear to you, the moment will come."

Fourteen

On Saturday Amanda tended the horses. As she saddled Sugar, her favorite mare, she swore. What had she possibly hoped to accomplish by nearly making love to him? Did she need to prove that there was nothing to feel, nothing to stew about? She broke into a canter. The wind was up; change was in the air. Clouds were coming over the tops of the pines as Amanda urged her horse into a gallop.

They followed the spine of the hill, down to the pasture, across the road, spewing crows from the spent cornfields as they raced past. She walked Sugar from the woods, past the ruins of an ancient barn. A ray of light broke through the clouds and sliced over the door. She thought about her childhood as the mare picked her way over the undergrowth.

This was reality, home, family, solid earth beneath her. Yesterday afternoon was a crazy dream, a dangerous temptation. Some other woman had ignited under his touch. Amanda laughed softly to herself and tried to dismiss the reverie.

The horseback ride was cathartic, and she took another on Sunday, this time concentrating on her Friday morning presentation. She had been good, not too verbose, succinct, professional. When the group awarded her the account, David would see that she had a full life, that she was competent. Handling the mill project would also put them both under even more scrutiny. There could be no giving in to hormones once the construction was in full swing.

As she swung over the pastures, she half expected David to show up at the stable, or the crest of a hill. This time she ambled down the bridle trail and along the low rock wall that separated Sycamore Hill from River's Edge. She came within sight of the Lydon estate, within hearing distance of the tennis court. Under gray skies she spotted Jace playing mixed doubles. The man across the net wasn't David.

Before heading back to Wilmington Amanda made an overdue call on the ailing Maggie Lydon, matriarch of the neighboring family. The older woman was propped on the couch, but well enough to insist that Amanda stay for a cup of tea. Jace joined them in his tennis clothes and listened to his mother's family news. In addition to their own Sycamore Hill horses the Lydons raised cattle on a spread in Montana, always Maggie's favorite topic.

Jace mentioned his sister, who had left the carriage house to settle on the ranch. He talked of the cowboy who had stolen her heart. He talked of his tennis. Maggie asked about Amanda's parents and, over a second cup of tea, mentioned her new tenant. "Such a coincidence," she said.

"Yes," Amanda murmured.

"Here I am a member of the Historical Society, so thrilled about the future of the mill, and along comes the architect, interested in renting the carriage house. Then, lo and behold, who does the architect turn out to be but *your* David!"

"Not any longer, Mrs. Lydon."

"No, I guess not, but he's still as charming as ever. Remember the party I gave for the two of you that New Year's? Your mother was so upset that you'd eloped. However, both your parents grew to be very fond of him."

"It was a long time ago."

"Yes," she sighed, "I suppose it was. My own daughter's found herself a cowboy. Dory Lydon and our ranch manager, can you imagine? Children—even the grown ones—can still be full of mischief."

Mischief, Amanda thought. Maybe that was all it had been.

"I hope you're both over your bitterness," Maggie continued. "Jace has said that things have been quite pleasant between you. I hope so, Amanda dear. I never would have considered him as a tenant under any other circumstances."

Amanda shook her head. "There's no bitterness. We're both getting on with our lives, that's all."

The Lydon matriarch waved a gnarled finger. "Wouldn't hurt either of you a bit to give it another go. You're both so full of life now, so successful."

"We've gone our separate ways."

"Fine, but just don't arrive at my age with a heart full of regrets. Jack Lydon and I had our ups and downs, but never anything we couldn't resolve. What a life we had together! And when the time comes, my ashes will be right out there with his under that huge Montana sky at the Rocker L."

"You even make that sound romantic."

"What's life unless you put your whole heart into it?"

Later, as Amanda left, she glanced at the carriage house, aglow at the bottom of the driveway. She stopped long enough to ponder her whole heart, then walked in the opposite direction along the bridle path and home to River's Edge.

She ate a quick supper with the Jimersons, scooped up Lipton and drove back to her town house. The rain started as she left, spitting fitfully against her windows, finally developing into a downpour.

Still she brooded over Friday. David had begged her to make love to him, then disappeared for the rest of the weekend. Abrupt departures weren't his style. They had always been hers, as he'd reminded her. David was the pensive one, the quiet man whose silences she'd faced after her solitary walks. He'd never come after her, but he'd always been there on her return. Often she'd find him at his drawing board immersed in work. Work as a panacea was something he'd picked up from her, but even that had failed to cure their mutual illness. Arguments might have resolved something.

"Hindsight," she muttered as she pulled the remains of a quiche from her refrigerator. She ate on the couch and watched a Katharine Hepburn classic with Lipton, rueing the moment she'd let David Smith back into her life.

The workweek began with soggy earth but sunny skies. Amanda tried to concentrate on new business and not the eternal wait for the Oakhurst powers to make their decision. Her co-workers seemed disgustingly cheerful. Karen, who kept fresh flowers on her desk, had added a bouquet on top of Amanda's filing cabinet. Marco took to playing classical music and waltzed his boss around his workroom when she made the mistake of entering to check on a layout.

"It must be the rubber-cement fumes," he said when she protested.

"I think it has more to do with your lopsided optimism. Please let go of me."

He did. "You could use more optimism. What's to gain from moping around, biting your nails and getting migraines?"

Amanda looked at her fingers. "Marco, this is business. Somebody has to take it seriously."

"I take business very seriously. I was referring to your lusting after your ex-husband."

"I am not lusting!"

"Pining, then. Sorry."

"I admit I'm not myself. Maybe I'm tense, but it's the account, this interminable waiting to hear something."

"We've waited before, for bigger fish than this one." Marco smiled innocently. "If we do land this fish, what then? What are you going to do about the architect?"

"There's nothing *to* be done about him."

If she'd meant there was nothing to be done about getting him out of her mind, erasing the memories of moments in his arms, or dismissing the erratic swing of her moods when she thought about the situation, if she'd meant it was impossible to dismiss how firmly he had planted himself back in her life, then she was right on the mark.

Five more minutes in the presence of her art director would unleash all of it, and rather than confess to feelings she was loath to admit even to herself, she returned to her office and closed the door.

The following day she wrote copy for thirty-second radio spots for a men's store, drummed her desk with her fingers and reviewed the drive-time prices being charged by the biggest radio stations to place the ads. "I'm good at this, damn good," she muttered, as if someone were about to disagree.

She took the sales manager of WESD to lunch, and over a chef's salad she bought three months' airtime for her client. As she ate, she thought about the Conservation Council.

By Wednesday she was obsessed. At that moment were Oakhurst, the Brachmans and John Wilkins reviewing the presentations, making their decision? David Smith would have opinions, too, whether he voiced them or not. It didn't matter whether he talked to the committee. After six years of having an entire country between them, and skills honed by the best in the business, Amanda still saw her ex-husband as sitting in judgment of her.

The call came at four o'clock. Rather than buzz her phone, Karen came to Amanda's office to say that John Wilkins was on the line. She gave her boss a thumbs-up gesture and closed the door as she left.

"John," Amanda began, "I was hoping to hear from you before the end of the day."

"Then I'm glad I called," he replied pleasantly. "And I won't leave you in suspense. We've given the account to Samuels Associates. Your prices were competitive, but we felt their presentation was a little closer to the mark. You did have some outstanding ideas, however, and I wish you well. I'm sure you and your agency will do fine in this market.''

She discussed the presentation in her best professional voice and then thanked him. Hollowness replaced the churning in her chest. Disappointment tore at her composure. It was over. After the stewing and sweating, the work and determination, not to mention the interminable waiting, a one-minute conversation canceled the dream. Her chest hurt and her throat burned.

Amanda glared at the phone. Samuels Associates was a bastion of male supremacy, large, successful, fail-safe to a client's mind, boring and unimaginative to hers.

Defeat exhausted her. She sat at her desk unable to clear her mind, wanting to be anywhere but where she was. After she gathered her briefcase and blazer, she opened her door. Marco was sitting on the edge of Karen's desk, and both employees looked at her hopefully.

Amanda shook her head. ''Sorry, guys, we lost to Samuels.''

Marco swore under his breath and stood up. ''Leaving?''

Amanda nodded. ''Close up at five. I'll see you both in the morning.''

Marco followed her as far as the sidewalk. ''What are the chances I could talk you into dinner and a movie?''

''Thanks, anyway.''

''My own tortellini—''

''Food isn't the answer. I want some time alone.''

"All right. It was a tough break, but we gave it our best shot, boss. Nobody's going to starve."

"This wasn't about starving, Marco."

He touched her arm. "Are you ready to admit what it was really about?"

Fifteen

David sat at his drafting table, staring at a roll of tissue overlay paper. Guilt was a wasted emotion, yet that was what he felt, guilt and an odd sense of relief. Samuels Associates had designed an excellent campaign. They'd won the account fair and square. He tapped his pencil on the drafting table, willing himself to concentrate.

"Impossible," he muttered as he crumpled the paper and picked up the phone.

Thirty minutes later, on a tip from Marco, David knocked on the open kitchen door of River's Edge. When no one answered, he let himself in, nearly tripping over the sleeping calico cat.

"Lipton, you're a good sign. Your mistress must be around somewhere," he said as he spotted a note still propped next to a basket of muffins.

Amanda,
Thanks for tending the horses. Scott and family will be back Friday evening. We'll be home Sunday.

Hannah

David walked the bridle trail, the pasture and finally the meadow bordering the Brandywine River at the bend of the farm. He caught sight of Amanda well before she knew she was being watched.

The woman rode like a dream, rode the way she did everything else, for that matter. She was astride a Thoroughbred gelding and had the horse in an easy gait, her posture correct, her style confident. She wore a handsome cotton pullover and chaps over her jeans. Her hair tumbled from under her riding hat. The sight of her made him ache all over, the way he had every damn night he'd crawled into bed alone.

The soft earth was puckered with leaves and smelled of autumn as the Thoroughbred's hooves kicked up the dirt. She stopped where the meadow opened to the river, and sat in the saddle watching the water rush over the rocks. As he approached, the horse whinnied suddenly, and Amanda pivoted in the saddle.

David kept walking, willing his heart to stop its thunder. He strode as though he were pacing out a potential architectural site, both hands in the pockets of his khakis. The collar of his ancient tweed sport jacket was up, and pens and glasses peeked from the chest pocket of his flannel shirt. As he reached the horse and rider, he kicked one of his work boots against the other, dislodging mud. He pointed to Dancer's tracks. "Thought I might find you here."

"You were looking?"

"Marco said you'd gone for the day. I saw the note in the kitchen. Here for the night?"

"Tending the horses."

"How about tending your emotions?"

"If you're thinking about repeating last Friday's offer, I have no intention—"

"Neither do I."

For the first time their glances met. David took the rein drooped along the gelding's neck. "Get down, Dazzle."

"Go back to work. I'm going to ford the river."

He kept his hold on the rein. "Come down, or I'll come up."

Amanda slid from the saddle. "This is a waste of time. I don't want to talk, either."

"Then I will. One of us has to mention the fact that you lost the mill account. I'm sorry."

She inhaled sharply. "I didn't stand a chance once they found out about us. Even if they swore not to let it influence them, how could they help it? How could Wilkins not worry about how it would look when grants were involved?"

"The committee put a lot of thought into that decision. Why stick me with the blame? Dazzle, you lost fair and square. The group from Samuels was better, more suited to their needs."

"Samuels is full of just what they wanted—middle-aged men."

David watched the river and then turned to her. "Talented men. They have experience at this. Their presentation was excellent."

"Mine wasn't?"

He laughed sardonically. "Who would have ever thought I'd be in a position to judge you professionally? Yours was very, very good. All the competitors' were. The board chose the one most matched to what they think they want. It's as simple as that. Stop acting as though you couldn't compete."

"I know perfectly well how to compete in this business."

"And you don't think I've known that since your first little advertising job in Princeton? Since you took Manhattan by storm while I sat at a drafting table fourteen hours a day? You don't think these weeks have been a constant reminder of your professional Midas touch?" David's frustration kept his heart hammering.

"I certainly lost the touch today."

David took her by her shoulders as his complexion deepened. "You lost. Why, after all these years, is it still so damn important to prove to me that you can't fail?"

"Can't fail! Don't you know? Work is the *only* place where I didn't fail. I made you miserable, every month got worse. I was never what you wanted. I was never who you wanted. At least at the agencies I was doing something right. I was appreciated."

"Did you ever know what I wanted? Did you ever take the time to find out what I needed?"

"I tried! You didn't want me or the money."

"You resented having to make it."

"Not as much as you resented having to take it."

He put his hand along her cheek. "What did you want, Amanda? What did you want that we couldn't have gone after together? Why was it so important to start over without me?"

"You didn't want me." She turned and put her hands on the saddle, but as she lifted her foot to the stirrup, he stopped her.

"There's no running away. Stay here and finish it." He tugged her back down on the grass. "We came so close Friday, so close I almost forgot what wedges have been driven between us."

"You had a whole life without me. You had graduate school, and I was in the way. Your classmates shared your life. I didn't. You were never home."

"There wasn't anybody in the apartment to come home to."

"Because I was out working to pay for all of it."

"Amanda, could it be that you were out proving that you didn't need me any more than you thought I didn't need you?" Under his breastbone the interminable ache began to radiate. The slow, burning grief that had dissipated only after years of trying to forget had returned.

"I found something that made me feel valuable. I made money for you, for us."

"By then there wasn't any us."

"You didn't want us. You didn't want me." She blinked and swiped at her eyes.

"Always, always I wanted you, but I couldn't admit it." David forced his voice to steady. "Every bonus you brought home was a constant reminder that I wasn't keeping up my end of the bargain. I was miserable. How on earth were we going to please each other when we couldn't even please ourselves?"

Inside Amanda burned. David's words rang true, and a hundred memories crowded into her head. She looked at him without a shred of pretense. "I did want to please you more than anything. Can't you see that we're proof of how dangerous that is? When that doesn't work, there's nothing left but to make yourself happy."

"And you were determined to be left with something, so your work became the substitute. Did I push you away? Was our life together so bad? Am I forgetting? I kind of liked peanut butter and jelly for dinner."

"That last year it wasn't the peanut butter and jelly. We were naive about too many things."

"There was pleasure along the way." As he spoke, David's grip on her shoulder loosened. Through the cotton she felt the warmth of his hand as if he'd just touched her skin. "Friday was a reminder of that pleasure, Dazzle." He ran his hand gently to her breast. She put her fingers over his.

"Friday would have been a mistake for both of us. You knew it then, or you wouldn't have left."

He pulled her to him, his face next to hers. "Your reason was sound back then, but that reason's gone. You lost the account. There's nothing standing in the way but our past, our damn, interminable past. In three weeks you haven't been this honest. You haven't let yourself."

"I'm not worried."

"Maybe you should be. Or maybe it's too late for worry. Friday I came out here and found you to prove something to myself."

Amanda stepped back and moved his hand.

"You needed me that rainy Sunday when you saw our picture in the paper. My God, Amanda, just hearing you say the words was like salve on a blister. You needed me, and you hated it. Can you see how I felt in school? Do you understand? Friday I wanted to prove that I could get you to make love to me, that you'd needed me again."

"That's not what you told me."

"It doesn't matter. My motives were completely self-centered until I listened to you. You thought about more than yourself last weekend. You thought of me."

"It's been tough to think of much else."

Impulsively he cupped her face and kissed her. "There was so much that I loved about you."

The warmth of his hands permeated her cheeks, her ears. Under her hat her scalp tingled. Love. She hadn't so much as thought about the emotion in years. Decades. Centuries. He stepped forward and seemed to mold to her as he kissed her. She felt the supple leather of her chaps against his thighs and the warmth of her breasts against his shirt. His hands caught the rim of her hat as her fingers pressed his spine.

"David."

He stepped back to look into her eyes. "There's nothing in the way, Dazzle."

"Except reality." With a small jump she jammed her boot into the stirrup and hoisted herself into the saddle. "I'm thinking of you now. Leave me alone. You'll be better off. We both will."

David looked up at her. "When it happens—and it will—it'll be love we're making, the kind we had once before being true to ourselves became more important than being true to each other."

Amanda looked down at his handsome face. "You of all people should know that until you're true to yourself you can't be good for anyone else. You're restless and dissatisfied."

He stroked the horse's mane. "Amanda, darling, restless and dissatisfied is exactly how I've found you. I suspect you're out here today because you lost the Oakhurst account and failed in front of me. That thought is so devastating that it drove you right out of the one place you thought you were safe—your office."

Her color deepened, and with a sharp tug on the reins she urged the horse away from him. "G'yap!" The horse trotted, then broke into a canter. She left David behind on the riverbank and cantered away from him across the meadow. She never looked back.

Even before she reached the wooded trail her retreat embarrassed her. It was no different from her sudden exits from their apartments. A stomp down West Eighty-second Street, a dash across the Princeton campus, a ride along the Brandywine—none of them solved a thing, none of them helped rid Amanda of her sense of failure or feeling of loss.

To cool the horse she walked him home to the stables. It would be just like her ex-husband to be lounging against the paddock rail as she came up the cart path. She had always had to face him after those painful retreats. David had never had any other place to go any more than she did.

Anticipation kept her pulse swift as Dancer made his way home to the stable where she and David had made such glorious love in another life. She relived the moments, remembering most clearly how she'd loved him. She arrived breathless from her reverie, but there was nothing but the sound of the horse's hooves over the cobblestones to break the silence. She curried Dancer and put him out to pasture with the others, then fed and watered them all. No David. No tricks. The dull ache of disappointment refused to leave her.

She went into the tack room to put her riding hat back in its place. As she peeled off her chaps, a familiar voice, full of the playfulness and passion she couldn't dismiss, murmured, "Keep going."

Sixteen

"It's the one thing we gave equally, the one way we could always communicate," David whispered as he watched her. His heart thundered so hard that he heard nothing but his pulse. She kept her back to him, the chaps still in her hands.

"It was never better than in here, that hot, steamy Fourth of July. You knew exactly what you wanted and so did I." His ribs stretched over his lungs as he filled them. "Trying to forget hasn't done us any good."

She dropped the chaps, and he caught his breath. "We need to remember."

Still silent, she put her hands to her waist in front of her so that he couldn't see. His own fingers scrambled over his belt buckle. Slowly, it seemed in time to his hardening body, she pulled her sweater up. Unbelievably she tugged it over her head, catching her hair. An incredulous, joyful David fumbled with his shirt buttons. She unfastened her bra and dropped it.

He was alive with desire, with his need to feel her skin, to hold her, to ignite what simmered. He stepped forward until his bare chest pressed her back, and cupped her breasts. Her softness was in such contrast to his rock-solid length that he sighed.

She purred as he kissed the nape of her neck, her shoulder and her ear. "You need this," he gasped. He turned her around and smiled at the expression he'd prayed he'd find. "Most of all, *I* need this." He traced the curve of her lip, the playful smile. "I haven't seen that expression in years."

"Tell me we know what we're doing, that we won't be sorry" were the first words she spoke.

"I've been sorry before. I may be sorry again. I gave up long ago trying to make sense of what feels right in my life." He couldn't think, and as he stepped from his jeans, he didn't want to.

"Later, maybe we'll both be sorry," she managed, yet caressing him all the while. "You were made for this," she whispered. Her softness made him weak, and his desire for her made him crazy.

The sun had topped the trees, but he wasn't chilled. He moved with her around the partition to the clean, empty stall and watched the dappled light play off her spine. Her sigh was as smooth and hot as brandy.

They rushed, unable or unwilling to wait. David held her head with one hand and deepened his kisses as he slid the other over her ribs, never still. He was dizzy with wanting nothing but the feel of her everywhere.

"The Jimersons are gone," she whispered. "Everyone's gone."

David nodded. "Touch me," he whispered back. "This is better than tears." He repeated her name. He kissed her temples and her eyes. "Look at me, Dazzle," he whispered, and while she stared back at the deepening desire in his eyes, he kissed her breasts. She arched her back again. "Sultry doesn't begin to describe you."

His own skin flamed as she kissed the soft curve of his shoulder, his chest, his mouth. She kissed and massaged with an urgency that left him gasping. Roughly he tugged her to the hay, their breathing rapid and evenly matched.

The glance into each other's eyes was more intimate than any of their caresses. "The minute I saw you in that satin I remembered how you felt, how my fingers used to tingle, how your breasts moved, how we slept. How we'll be now."

"Now," she repeated, as if she was oblivious to anything but the rough-smooth friction of their skin, the spiraling heat coursing through him. His hands moved over her, memorizing the fullness, the shallows. Amanda cried out and pulled him to her, unable to keep her own hands still.

He felt her shudder, his kisses deep and urgent, and his heart hammered against hers. Beneath him she shifted and guided him until they melded their rough urgency into matched rhythm. Every inch of him was alive, in tune with her, racing ahead, falling back. The heat became unbearable as she called him and clung to him. The moments were measured in heartbeats, and as she welcomed him, there was no thought in his head except what they were at that moment to each other.

Amanda snuggled as he pulled her in against the crook of his shoulder. "Dazzle," he sighed, "how did we lose this? Did I stop paying attention?''

"It's not enough to carry a relationship. It wasn't then. It wouldn't be now.'' She ran her hand over his palm, the calluses, looking at the blunt-cut fingernails. "You toughened up," she remarked gently.

"In some areas. I'm putting in a patio for a client. It's the best part of the day sometimes.''

"Where do we go from here?" she asked.

"Back into our clothes," David replied, supporting himself on one elbow. "Regrets?''

"My regrets lie with how I failed you.''

"You didn't *fail.*''

"You would have been happier with your work if you'd had less stress at home. You were the one meant for the shining future, not me. It was your future we were both supposed to be working for.''

"Lo and behold, you got involved in advertising and loved it.''

"As much as you hated it.''

"I hated that you weren't there for me. I hated being dependent on you. That doesn't mean you failed me, Amanda. It means I was more selfish than I should have been.'' He kissed her breast. "We were meant for a fresh start. Let this be it. Let something good come from losing the account.''

"Current business is the least of our problems. Stay.'' She moved her fingers through his hair as his cheek warmed her shoulder.

David sat up and continued to dress. "How about dinner at the inn?''

"Hannah left too much food. We can pull something together.''

"Are you afraid someone might see us, or are you too besotted to share me with the Chadds Ford public?"

Amanda wrestled the pullover back on, not bothering with the bra, and got back into her jeans. "Personally what we've just done is questionable enough. Even without the account, professionally it shows an incredible lack of judgment."

"What have we just done, Dazzle?" She pivoted, but he held her gently by the arm. "Personally, I mean." *Made love.* He knew she could feel it, sense it. "Do you have any idea? Was it just another swing around the dance floor to get each other out of our systems?"

"Maybe these are just more questions without answers."

They walked to the house together. At the kitchen she scooped Lipton into her arms with a Cheshire-cat smile.

"What's the grin for?"

She pulled a can of cat food from the pantry. "When I see you most of the time, you look like a bank president. Now your shirt's out, your hair's mussed, your socks are jammed into your pocket. Funny contrast, that's all."

He pulled her bra from his pocket. "My socks are on. This is what's off. You look wonderful without it, loose, free, incredibly sexy."

She grabbed it and handed him the can. "Feed the cat."

"What are you going to feed us?" he asked when Lipton was settled at his dish.

"You can decide. I need a shower. Why don't you rummage around in the refrigerator and put something together?" She cocked her head. "I assume in these years on your own you've improved your skill in the kitchen.''

''I assume since you haven't commented on my skill in the stable that some things needed no improvement whatsoever.''

She threw a dish towel at him and disappeared up the back staircase by the laundry room.

Amanda's bathroom adjoined the two east bedrooms on the second floor. As she soaped, she caught sight of the blurred, masculine image through the shower door. ''There are five bathrooms in this house. I suggest you find one that isn't occupied,'' she called loudly.

''Not a chance,'' David replied as he slid the frosted glass door back on its tracks. ''Where's your shock and moral outrage?''

Shampoo ran down her temple, and she jammed her eyes shut as she slid the door closed. ''It's a little late for that. False modesty was never my style.''

David slid it open again. ''The door was unlocked. I thought for sure that was an invitation.''

''Baloney. Scott fell in the shower when he was ten and Dad had to take the door off the hinges before he could get to him. Since then none of us showers with the door locked. You knew that, Mr. Ex-Husband.''

''You can't expect me to remember everything.'' He took off his clothes a second time.

''Your selective memory's going to get you into trouble.''

''Some things are worth forgetting, others worth remembering.''

''What, exactly, did you think I'd do when you sneaked in here?'' She stepped aside and made room for him.

"You've been giving me startled expressions for two weeks. I thought for sure I'd get a healthy scream out of you."

She scrubbed her hair. "I've seen *Psycho* so many times, even Norman Bates in here wouldn't scare me."

David slid his hand over her shoulder, and she weighed pleasure against pain. That this one man was the source of both still mystified her. With warm, wide fingers he took the soap and continued for her.

"I was expecting that, too," she murmured.

"Then you won't be disappointed." He lathered her breasts playfully, then put the soap back in her hand and brought it to his chest. Holding her wrist, he guided her in slow circles. "Got the idea?"

"I thought this afternoon was *once* around the dance floor."

"The night is young. Anything can happen."

Seventeen

Freshly scrubbed and properly dressed, they headed for the kitchen and ate an early supper—a decent meal David put together of chicken and peas. Amanda's contributions were two potatoes stuck in the microwave oven for eight minutes. Sunset slit the clouds and skimmed the treetops as they cleared their plates.

Amanda stood at the sink. "I think we've taken this about as far as it can go."

"You don't believe that."

"Perhaps I should have said, we've taken this about as far as I intend to let it go. How about that?"

"You need to keep going, Amanda."

Her eyes flashed. "You have no idea what I need. You never knew."

He smiled, scraped his plate and put the stopper in the drain. He squirted detergent under the flowing water. "Now we're getting someplace."

"Stop doing the dishes."

"It gives me something to do with my hands. Hand me your plate and tell me what it was you needed that I never knew about."

"David, just because we've fooled around in the stable—"

"And the shower."

"And the shower. That still doesn't mean we have anything more than we had in our former relationship."

"Marriage, Dazzle. The former relationship was a marriage."

"We made a mockery of the word."

"You are as infuriating now as you were then." He washed and rinsed one plate.

"Stop!"

"The dishes or the analysis?" He handed her a clean dish towel and the plate.

"Both."

"If memory serves me correctly, you're on the verge of throwing something or stomping into the night. I suggest the latter. It's safer out here on the farm than it was in Manhattan, so I won't sit here eating my heart out with worry while you're gone. Go ahead. Take a walk. I'll be here when you get back."

Amanda rubbed the plate with the linen towel. "You never worried. Nothing ever fazed you."

When the silence became unbearable, he sighed. "You never knew."

She put down the dry plate without looking at him. "I'm not about to throw anything or run out of the house. I'm asking nicely for you to go. This whole afternoon has been overwhelming. We shouldn't have done what we did. It was foolish and impetuous."

"You're at your best when you're impetuous."

"I'd like to be alone, please."

"You've been alone for six years." The last of the water drained from the sink, and he wiped his hands. "Regret's a waste of energy. It's done, darling Amanda. It's too late for retreat. It used to work like a charm, didn't it? All that silence and noncommunicating kept us going most of that last year together. Separate lives, separate friends, separate goals."

"Divorce was the best thing for both of us. Look how well we've done without each other."

David pulled her into his arms and pressed her against him until he felt her catch her breath. "Then why does this feel so right?"

"Because of the challenge or the denial. Who can say? One physical act doesn't change anything. We're not kids out at the mill. Stop focusing on how we started and remember how we ended. *Those* feelings are every bit as real. We failed, and I put that failure behind me." She pushed away. "You should never have come out here last week with that champagne. You never should have come out here today. You've destroyed your relationship with Patsy because of us."

"There isn't any *us*, Dazzle. Not yet. Now that you can't use the account as an excuse, don't throw Patsy into your cockeyed reasoning."

She tried to turn, but he took her arm. "No one's taken your place, much as you hoped otherwise." He put his face to her ear, as if they weren't alone. "I know your body like I know my own. Maybe this afternoon satisfied your curiosity, but it hasn't begun to satisfy mine."

"If you stay, you'll be disappointed."

He pushed her gently out at arm's length. "In you? In what you've become? Give me the chance to discover that. Give *us* a chance to settle it."

"If you had any sense at all, you'd accept the fact that we don't matter to each other anymore."

"I don't believe that any more than you do."

"All I know is that I haven't had a moment's peace since you waltzed back into my life."

David kissed the bridge of her nose. "Then we're even."

They made it through the brewing and drinking of coffee with only small talk. She rambled on about Maggie Lydon's health, about growing up with Jace and Dory, the love of horses both families shared. She spoke of the trails on their properties, the mare she rode most regularly, and Hank Jimerson's expertise. The two of them settled in the living room, a plate of cookies between them.

David took one. "Did you know Maggie's a member of the Historical Society? I suppose your parents are, too."

"We all are."

"Small world."

"Life out here runs in small circles. Do you visit with her much?"

"When I can." He smiled. "That was some party she threw for us way back when."

"You were a nervous wreck."

"Too much blue blood and not enough blue collars."

"You've come a long way, David."

"So have you." He drained his coffee mug. "Did you ride much in Washington?"

She snapped on a lamp. "Some."

"Who'd you leave behind?"

"No one. You're impertinent. You know that?"

"I can't see that I'll get any answers unless I ask some questions."

Amanda looked into her coffee. "Why are the answers so damn important?"

"Because you are, Dazzle. You hotfooted it out of New York with a clean slate. Newly divorced, fresh start. It stands to reason that you'd flee from Seattle for the same reasons you left New York."

"I didn't flee. Hargrave and Morton transferred me to their West Coast office. I left the East with a big chunk of my life in turmoil. Seattle was a proving ground. Stop looking for skeletons in my closet. Washington State was wonderful. I worked hard and they rewarded me."

"And back you came—for business reasons."

"Yes. Is that so hard to accept? As I got to know the business, I became more interested in running my own firm and Wilmington, not Seattle, was the logical place."

"Financial backing?"

"I have a loan from my father."

"You wouldn't take a dime in the beginning."

"I grew up," she replied quietly.

"The turmoil must have settled."

"Of course. Didn't yours?" She watched him hesitate, stirred by the range of emotion in his features. When had he grown so perceptive? Where had he garnered the insight? Why was he still so irritatingly handsome? And how, after all this time, could he still be such a conundrum?

He sighed. "You give new meaning to the word *turmoil*. I thought mine was settled, too, until that April afternoon."

Amanda got up from the couch and walked to the window. She sat on the deep-set sill and looked out at the settling darkness. As David came to her, a sudden flush crept up from her breasts and washed her jaw.

David's reflection, distorted by the panes, moved over the dark window. For six years he'd been applying his skills to design and labor. The work had hardened him physically. His shoulders were broad, his stomach flat, more tapered than before. Pleasure tightened her breasts as she thought of him naked and playful.

He touched her jaw where the color was deepest. "Amanda, you've come back alone with no one in your life but your professional colleagues. Where I failed, nobody else has succeeded, either. I don't know why that cheers me."

She turned from the window, and her flush deepened. "One broken heart is enough."

"There were two. Six years is a long time not to fall in love again."

"I didn't go out there to fall in love."

"No, you went out there to forget, to put a continent between yourself and your first try at it. Then when the all-clear signal sounded in that heart of yours, you came home."

Amanda got to her feet. "You don't honestly believe that."

"Tell me what to believe."

"Believe that I put heartache aside. I worked night and day until Hargrave made me account executive of clients I'd only dreamed of representing in New York.

Believe that I learned well from the best in the business, and believe that I brought that expertise back with me."

"The Mendenhalls must have been happy to have you back."

"My family's important," she replied.

"Financial backing?"

"No handouts, David. Why is money always an issue?"

"Because we never had any."

"Taking from my family back then would have proved that I was as dependent as they thought I'd be. I learned a lot supporting you."

"God, I hated it."

She laughed ruefully. "At least I know you didn't marry me for tuition money."

"Dazzle—"

"Forget it. Going to work was the best thing that could have happened. I learned a lot about the advertising business and even more about myself, maybe even some things about my family."

"That they were right?"

"Their concerns were justified, just as your family's were."

"My family cared about you, Amanda." His voice was mellow. "You know I'm right. Your way of dealing with stress was to shut me out, midsentence. A walk anywhere felt better than facing my opinion."

"Facing your anger, your disapproval," she whispered. "Your rejection."

Amanda put her hand out as if to stop him, but he took it and pressed it slowly against his shirt. The warmth began again to surround her heart. "*Your* rejection," he countered.

There were questions in her eyes, but she changed the subject. "My father will be glad to hear you're doing so well. You should have kept in touch with him. He was interested in your career."

"Clean breaks don't come by keeping in touch with ex-fathers-in-law."

She nodded. "You're right. Forgive me."

He covered her hand with his and put his free arm across her shoulder. "It's time for forgiveness."

Hearing him say it made her heart dance. She needed him to stay. She needed to continue, to make sense of the electricity still surging between them. Making love to him had raised more questions than it had answered, but she'd walk from Wilmington to Seattle before she'd admit to any of it.

She raised her face to look at him, and he kissed her. It was impetuous and unexpected. His lips parted slightly in surprise, and she parted hers. The feel of him bathed her in false security.

Eighteen

In six years David had honed to perfection the fine art of living for the moment. As his pulse began to pound, he sensed that Amanda might never repeat the recklessness of this day. For now, however, for whatever reasons, she was responding to her own needs. It would be delusion to think that this was more than the chemistry they'd always shared. Still it was enough to keep his blood racing. It was enough to give him hope.

"Weren't we just talking about clean breaks?" she asked.

"It was just a kiss."

"You don't believe that for a minute."

"Yes, I do. I didn't at first, but you're right. This is what we've needed, this day, this proof that we can live in the same town, that we've gone on with our lives. Odd, but making love to you feels like a clean break."

Hurt drifted in and out of her expression.

He looked at her, kissed her lightly and then smiled. "We might as well get all this desire out of our systems right now."

"You're making fun of me."

"Quite the contrary. I'm agreeing with you." He kissed her again. "Your approach is just what we need. Quick and fun."

He never intended to take it any farther. Convincing words were already a smoke screen for what had begun to simmer in the stable. There was only one reason why Amanda incited such passion in him, a reason he refused to consider.

Her expression was masked; she was lost in her own thoughts. At the moment he least expected it she cupped his face and kissed him back. He stood stockstill, feeling the heat of her hands on either side of his jaw, the sudden warmth of her breasts against his chest, her thighs against his.

His body betrayed him in a response so deep and true that he grabbed her for support.

"Stay," she moaned softly.

"Start from now with me, Dazzle. Give us another chance."

She was panting softly. "Don't you see that I've already given you everything? This is all there is, David." She smiled dreamily. "Isn't this enough? Isn't this what you've wanted all these weeks?"

What game was she playing? He smothered her words with his mouth.

"Let's go upstairs," she was whispering.

Her house, *her* stairs, *her* bedroom. *Her* game? He skimmed over her shirt and bra with his hand as she responded. Never still, he cupped one breast and then the other until she shuddered at his touch. What he could do with his thumb alone left her gasping. He turned off the single lamp, and the room filled with indirect light from the hall. Bits of dusk splashed through the windows.

David unbuttoned her shirt and savored his own pleasure. The shadows over the planes of her body played against his. Six years had been wonderful to her. He pressed his mouth to the pulse point at her throat, and she arched her back.

There was nothing quick, no desperate urgency as there had been in the stable. David caressed every inch of her as she removed his clothes. There was no going upstairs. They tumbled onto the soft couch, urging each other on, giving pleasure and taking more.

The intimacy was familiar, and David opened himself to Amanda's touch. "Remember," he groaned as she shifted beneath him, already moving with practiced hands.

There wasn't another woman on earth capable of making him feel the way she did. The revelation wove pain through the pleasure. Whether they let their passion thunder, or stayed playful, there was a part of Amanda he couldn't reach. There was a part of herself she wouldn't offer, just as he still held back part of himself.

They lay together on the down-filled sofa, dozing. When Amanda stirred, David looked at the tumble of sable hair and the curve of her hip. Moonlight dusted her spine. This had once been his. He sat up and pulled on his shirt against the ache.

"We should go up to bed," she murmured.

David got back into his clothes. "I'm not going to stay."

Amanda sat up sleepily. "I thought that's what you wanted."

"It's not the first time I was wrong."

She was obviously embarrassed. As he tucked in his shirt, she got up and floundered with her clothes. "Are you all right?"

"Sure."

She poked him playfully. "I got what I was after."

"I'm glad you weren't disappointed."

"David?"

He kissed her disheveled hair, aching to linger. "Curiosity can be dangerous. I'm leaving before it kills me."

"Just like that?"

"Let's call it a night while we're ahead of the game."

"You're angry."

"Will you ever see that it isn't anger?" He buttoned her shirt, and his knuckles played a dangerous game with the soft flesh he was covering.

"You certainly got what you came for, too."

David shook his head. "The hell of it is, I didn't."

She was quiet. It bolstered his confidence to sense her confusion. "I don't know what to say," she murmured.

"As always, there's as much in what you don't say as in what you do, as much in what you hold back as what you give. There's no point in rehashing this over breakfast tomorrow morning."

"And you don't hold anything back, David? You don't jump right for the sex, then waltz back into the night?"

"Believe it or not, I didn't come over here this afternoon with that on my mind."

"You could have fooled me."

"There's a phrase worth analyzing. Am I fooling you, or am I simply a fool? Are we deluding each other? Making love to you gives me glimpses of real intimacy. Problem is, darling ex-wife of mine, glimpses won't do anymore. I don't want to hold you and dream of what you could mean to me again. I don't want to touch you and spend the next day trying to figure out what went wrong, not unless you're as willing as I am to try again. Starting now."

"I've given you everything there is of me, everything I can."

He paused and watched her in painful silence. "Then I'm sorry. You broke my heart once, Amanda, back when that was all I had to give you."

The lamplight from the hall illuminated her surprise as she followed him across the room. He turned to her as he reached the foyer. "I'm not going to offer it up on a platter this time."

"And you didn't break mine?"

"Did I? You never told me." He kissed her quickly on her forehead. "I'm leaving before I drown. I'm testing waters too deep for any swimmer. Sleep well."

He let himself out the front door and forced himself to walk straight down the lane and over to the dark trail to Sycamore Hill. He ached to stay, to drink in the sight and smell of her, to rekindle memories of ecstasy and joy. What dreams there could be with her in his arms all night.

Instead, he shoved his hands into his pockets and shuddered in the cool night. He followed the bridle path to his carriage house, stopping once under the branch of an overhanging oak. Alone in the dark, he pressed his back against the trunk and stared into the night.

* * *

By the middle of the week Amanda's creativity had ebbed. Her temper was short and her disposition was as dark as the Brandywine's cold mud. She hadn't needed this misery six years ago, and she certainly didn't need it now. Forcing herself to concentrate on the work in front of her, she buzzed her art director.

"Give me five minutes, boss, then I'll be in," Marco replied.

She swiveled to the window and turned at the two sharp raps on her door. "Come in."

David Smith entered, then closed the door behind him and crossed the room in four easy strides. His color was high, his hair blown by the breeze off the river.

"I was expecting Marco," she managed.

"I told him to wait." He came to her and pressed both hands on her desk blotter. "Neither my head nor my gut's clear enough to think straight. It's affecting my work."

She flushed.

"From the glow in those cheeks I'll assume you're glad to see me."

"I told you, I was expecting Marco."

He shook his head. "Dazzle, if there were another man in your life, I'd understand you better. There isn't. There can't be. You've shown me too much of yourself these past weeks for me ever to think I've had competition. There may have been relationships along the way, but nothing as open and giving as what real love demands. It's beyond you. You failed with me, but I got as close as anyone."

Her heart refused to stop its racing. "David, you're out of line. It's the middle of the day."

He came around the desk to her. "I would prefer the middle of the night, but that's impossible at the moment. You misunderstand, Amanda. I know you don't love me. That's abundantly clear. Getting as close to you as anyone else has is hardly the brass ring. You've held love at arm's length since you were nineteen. No, make that twenty-one. We did have love in those first years."

"We've talked this over. Why have you burst in here like this?"

"The element of surprise works when all else fails. All else is failing."

"Then go back to work."

"I can't, and I need my work as much as you need yours, maybe more considering how far I've come. It's not the be-all and end-all of my life, though, not like yours. That's why I'm here. There's no point in discussing this over some quiet little dinner or buried in the depth of one of your couches. Anyplace more intimate than this office would make me want you all over again."

"We never should have—"

"Why? You let me into your arms because it was easier than talking. You'd do it again if you felt the urge, but frankly, that's the last place I need to be. You'll make love to me, Amanda, as long as you can keep reminding me of how awful we were together. Your constant dwelling on our past keeps you from facing the future."

His voice was barely raised above a whisper, but the shock of his words deepened her flush. "Please leave."

"Hear me out and then I'll go."

Amanda stared, wide-eyed and nearly speechless. "There can't be anything left."

"There's plenty. I feel more guilt than you know. I made you like this. I know that now. I can see it when you look at me and when you turn away. I've hardly thought of anything else this week but our conversations. Bits and pieces keep coming back—your anger, the sadness."

She half turned as he spoke, and he pulled her back around to face him. "David, this isn't necessary."

"Yes, it is. You're a wonderful, desirable woman with so much to give. Give it to someone. Love somebody, and make all this work of yours worthwhile. Don't let the mess we made ruin life for you. It was my fault as much as yours. Try again. Love again. It's worth the risk."

Her eyes were full of questions. "What an extraordinary thing to say," she murmured.

"Make someone happy."

"Why are you doing this?"

"There are other women out there, women like Patsy who deserve more than what I've been able to give." He tapped his heart. "I need to be free of you, rid of all of it. You need to be rid of it, too. Maybe we should have said that to each other long ago."

Her voice was thick, but she nodded. "Better late than never. I'm sorry, too. Please accept that."

His hand was already on the doorknob, and the moment he finished, he left.

Amanda sank farther into her chair. She listened to the soft click. It was over as suddenly as it had begun.

Nineteen

Days went by, then weeks. October had ignited the landscape with color. Amanda's parents were due back from Maine after a foliage trip through New Hampshire and a visit with Amanda's sister in Boston. Scott's children were looking forward to Halloween.

It had been three solid weeks since she'd seen or heard from David, weeks in which she'd done exactly what he'd told her to do: get on with her life. It didn't feel as if she were getting on with anything. It felt as though she were spinning her wheels.

Amanda had finished the first week with a business meeting at her CPA's office. She applied her usual steely determination to her social life and surprised him by accepting his impromptu offer of drinks and dinner downtown. That Saturday she surprised her brother and said yes to his suggestion of a date with a member of his law firm. They went out again in the middle of the week.

"Enjoying this new leaf you've turned over?" Marco asked one Monday morning as he set a plastic jack-o'-lantern on her desk.

"Yes. Hand me the file on Toys Galore, please" was her reply.

"You must have had quite a conversation with your architect when he came plowing into this office a while back."

"He's not my architect."

"With your professional conflict of interest out the window I thought for sure you two would strike up a sort of truce, and then who knows what might develop?"

"D'Abruzzi, one doesn't strike up anything with ex-husbands."

He dropped the file onto her blotter. "The eyes don't lie, especially yours. There's a sort of simmering hunger in them, overlying a long-buried hurt and unresolved longing."

"Enough melodrama. My simmering hunger's for lunch. You're crazy."

"No, I'm Italian. I know about passion and longing and all that unspoken regret. Truce is in the air. Don't blow it this time by going out in the real world and hoping for love to knock you over the head." With that he disappeared into his own office.

Falling in love—completely, madly—with someone else would have been the perfect solution. She drummed her fingers on the file folder and wondered why she hadn't taken the time or made the effort in the years without David.

Dinners here and there, a movie, the usual quips from Marco, didn't begin to fill the void. Amanda stewed and fretted over the fact that David Smith had left one in the first place, that after all this time he'd somehow managed to make his absence felt so deeply.

She had another Sunday lunch with Maggie Lydon. Jace made an appearance at dessert and asked if he'd blundered by renting the carriage house to her ex-husband. "We just finished splitting some logs, and I couldn't get him within fifty yards of here."

She dismissed his worry and the furtive glance of her hosts. "Don't go speculating, Mrs. Lydon."

"I'd be delighted to have something to speculate *on*, my dear."

Three days later, a month after David strolled out of her office, he strolled into Bradley's Tavern, a local restaurant. She was at a table with Marco, who cocked his head at the change in her expression, then turned around to see what had made her flush.

"Should have guessed," he said as he raised his hand.

"Stop waving!"

David spotted them and snaked his way through the tables. His smile was thin, his eyes troubled.

"There's always room at my table for a successful architect," Marco said as he offered a chair.

David patted Marco's shoulder and turned to Amanda. "Did you get your brother's message? He tried calling you at your house."

His expression made her heart leap. "No. Marco and I came here right from the office."

David put his hand on her arm. "Maggie Lydon's taken a turn for the worse, Dazzle."

"Her heart again?"

David nodded. "Complicated by the arthritis."

Amanda half rose, but David moved his hand to her shoulder. "Finish your dinner. There's nothing you can do at the moment. They've gotten her into intensive care at the medical center. Jace is there. He's called his sister. Dory's on her way."

"From Montana? Oh, David, this is serious."

The architect nodded.

Marco's plate was empty. "If you need tomorrow off, I can cover for you."

"I have a client lunch."

"My Brooks Brothers tie is always ready."

She smiled, grateful for the humor. "I'll let you know. Right now I'd like to see Jace, find out what I can do." She rifled through her purse. "My car keys are in here somewhere."

Marco said something to David, and he put his hand back on her arm. "I'll drive you to Sycamore Hill. Jace may have come home."

"If not, I'm going into Wilmington—the hospital."

"I'll take you."

Tears filled her eyes. "Thanks."

It was after one o'clock in the morning when David swung his Jeep into the winding drive of River's Edge and followed Amanda's taillights to the front door. Three cups of hospital coffee had frazzled his nerves and burned his stomach, but he was awake enough to have seen her through the first tense hours, and driven her back to her car at the tavern. From there, he'd let her drive herself no farther than the farm.

As he parked, he leaned his head on the steering wheel. Four weeks without her had been hell, almost as frustrating as the September weeks with her. He'd developed a permanent knot in his chest and a recurring dream. Amanda was on the stairs at the Advertising Council ball, all gossamer again, and candlelight. She walked toward him, but as he reached her, she blinked without recognizing him and continued into the crowd. When he turned to find her, she was always gone.

He took it as an omen to leave her alone once and for all. Time would heal him again, as it had the first time. The trouble with time, with laying one day in front of the next, was that the future lay out before him like a wasteland. It put the rest of his life on hold, as if he couldn't muster the energy to tackle anything else.

The previous Sunday, after piling logs with Jace, when he was sure Amanda had finished her visit with Maggie, he'd gone up to the big house with his rent check.

"You wouldn't join us," Maggie had said.

"It was appropriate."

"*Appropriate* won't get you anywhere."

"Actually, I wanted to discuss breaking my lease. Under the circumstances—"

"Circumstances? Lease breaking is serious business. I assume you've found yourself still in love with Amanda. Permit me to offer some unsolicited advice. You're wasting gorgeous days and empty nights. No doubt you're letting your creativity languish, while you live on nothing but the determination to see this relationship with my very confused young neighbor finished. The future belongs to both of you, David."

"Separate futures," he'd muttered.

"That's for the two of you to settle. Moving won't settle it. If I thought distance was what you two needed, I'd send you to the Rocker L for a week. Face her. Soon, for both your sakes.''

Maggie Lydon's lecture had only increased the ache. And now! He could have managed to keep Amanda at arm's length at one of Jace's tennis matches, some party of Marco's, even overlapping professional obligations. None of those would have presented him with the exhausted, grieving, vulnerable woman who was now fumbling with her house key.

The cold night air smelled faintly of wood smoke as they went into the dark house. A single lamp burned on the foyer table. He had surprised her here in his socks. He'd lectured her in the room down the hall and made love to her on the overstuffed sofa. Love? Passion, curiosity, desire were more like it. He could come up with half a dozen names for what it was, only one for what it wasn't. It wasn't love.

"Can you sleep?" he asked as she leaned against the wall.

"Yes. I'll stay upstairs, then go into the office tomorrow. Jace can reach me there if there's any change in his mother's condition. I'll come back out here after work. Dory's plane will be in by then.''

"She'll be glad to have your help.'' David's chest ached. He longed to crush her to him as she pursed her lips and looked at the ceiling to keep the tears from spilling.

Amanda brushed at her eyes. "This isn't unexpected, of course, but there's something so final about losing Mrs. Lydon. Her generation is going.''

He touched her hair. "It puts us in charge, forces responsibility.''

"Real life," she murmured.

"Isn't always what we've planned," he added as he forced himself to withdraw his hand. "Get some sleep."

"Thanks for following me home."

"It wasn't out of my way."

Something flickered in her expression, which he read as disappointment. He was too tired and wrung out himself to stand there and speculate on what—if anything—was going on behind her wide, sad eyes.

As she climbed the stairs, David returned to his car. He started his ignition as a single light came on in the bedroom above the flagstone porch. It had been their bedroom in another life. Maggie Lydon's passing would fill this house and Sycamore Hill. Family and neighbors he'd known briefly would descend again. Amanda would turn to them for emotional support, and once again he'd be the outsider, the Pittsburgh kid who'd swept their Amanda briefly off her feet.

Twenty

Two days later Amanda took Marco up on his offer to run the office in her absence. Maggie Lydon had died that afternoon, with her sister, brother-in-law and children beside her.

Overnight the houses had filled with family. Amanda's sister arrived with her parents. Dory Lydon had arrived from Montana with Alec McDowell, the Lydon ranch foreman whom everyone referred to as "Dory's cowboy." At Sycamore Hill Amanda's reunion with her childhood friend was bittersweet.

She marveled at the support Alec offered Dory and envied the ease with which she turned to him when the circumstances that had brought them all together threatened to overwhelm her. With the housekeeper attending to the constant phone calls and visitors, Amanda helped Dory make up beds and arrange rooms so that the elderly Lydon aunt and uncle and a set of cousins could stay in the main house with her. For propriety Alec bunked with Jace in his converted caretaker's cottage.

"We'll all be up here at the top of the hill," Dory added. "That way all this chaos won't disturb the tenant in my old carriage house. *The tenant.* Seems a funny way to refer to your ex-husband."

Amanda left Dory to Alec and her family and started toward the bridle path when she caught sight of David getting out of his car in front of his cottage. She tried not to think about how it still startled her to run into him, how it felt as though fingers clutched her heart when he touched her. He waved her over. The weeks of outdoor work had been good to him.

"Are you all right?" he asked when she was within earshot.

She nodded.

"Your parents are back?"

"Yes, they brought Lisa with them."

David nodded. "When the time's right, I'll renew old acquaintances. I'm going riding later with Jace, Alec and Scott. Maybe I'll stop by to see them when I return. Do they know I'm here?"

"They've known for a while."

"From you?"

"I might have mentioned it." The beginning of a smile startled her.

"Should I read something into your expression? You haven't done much smiling lately."

"You tend to come up in family conversations. They realize you've been very supportive these past few days. Thank you."

"From them?"

"From me."

* * *

David smiled back at her. "I was part of this once."

"It was hard for you, back then."

"It was hard to live up to expectations."

"I loved you the way you were." Her eyes widened.

Unconsciously David straightened at her use of the word. He laughed. "You look astonished, as if that terrifying word fell out of your mouth all by itself."

"You make me think about it too much, about the past."

"I'm no longer interested in the past."

Amanda looked up the hill. "The future will be different out here now."

"Maggie would be the first to tell you that life goes on." He touched her. It was impossible to stand within inches of her and not ache to hold her against him. For a moment she looked as if the ache was mutual.

She took his hand, held it between hers and then let it go. "Times like these make us all philosophers. I do agree with you, David. The past is behind us."

He forced himself to concentrate on the subject at hand. "And not a day too soon. What about tomorrow? Are you all set for the service?"

"Yes. I'll go with my sister and the rest of my family."

"Of course."

"Dory and Alec will take the ashes back to the ranch when they fly back out. There'll be another memorial service out there for all the cowboys, the manager and his family. Everybody at the Rocker L."

"Is there anything I can do for either family?"

"Dory and Jace are trying very hard to let you have your privacy, so this doesn't interfere."

"I hope it's occurred to someone that Maggie Lydon touched my life, too." He looked at the sky. "She was such an outdoors person. Somehow this wonderful weather seems appropriate." He lowered his voice. "The last time I talked with her at length she gave me hell for doing the *appropriate* thing, for even using the word."

"You got to know her well?"

"We had you in common, Dazzle. She thought I was too restless, as if I was trying to get you out of my system."

Amanda turned slowly for the path and David reached for her. The simple gesture brought tears to her eyes. She bowed her head, which only made them spill.

"Dazzle?"

"It's all right. I'm just exhausted, physically and emotionally. It doesn't help to dwell on all of the Lydon observations and advice she heaped on me this fall."

"You, too?" He felt her shiver under his touch.

"None of us escaped the Lydon philosophy."

"Which was to grab life and make the most of it."

She nodded and blinked. "I know."

"Are you?" Compassion and impatience filled him. Why couldn't he get on with his life the way he'd insisted she should? How long could he wait for this woman?

"I thought I was." Then she glanced at him. "My family's waiting," she murmured.

Desire taunted him, but his expression softened. "I won't keep you, then."

* * *

The memorial service was beautiful in its simplicity. The fieldstone building was lined with stained-glass windows that shimmered in the autumn sunlight. Although friends, neighbors and business associates had already begun to fill the country church, David whispered to the usher and walked alone down the center aisle.

Heads turned, and he imagined whispered conversations. *Isn't that Amanda Mendenhall's ex-husband? Doesn't that guy look just like the Pittsburgh kid who talked Amanda into eloping years ago?* He fought the urge to turn and nod or whisper back, *Yes, it's me.* He seated himself behind the Lydons. Jace turned briefly and nodded. Diagonally across the aisle the Mendenhalls filled the front pews. Although he kept his gaze forward, he felt their glances, as well.

There was a choir. The minister introduced Maggie's favorite hymn. As the mourners sang, David glanced at the baptismal font where he and Amanda had stood one weekend afternoon for her niece's christening. Eight years ago? She'd joked about Sunday school in the basement. The minister had mentioned the ceremonies of life.

Now the same minister repeated the phrase as the organ stopped and he proceeded with the service. David focused on the grays and blues of the granite walls, the Gothic arches and flickering flame of the vigil light. The windows behind the alter shone as Jace got up to offer his mother's eulogy.

David glanced across the aisle. Amanda was between her sister and father. Her hair gleamed and light caught the wool of her blue jacket. She had on kid gloves and was holding a handkerchief to her eyes. He watched her until his vision blurred. He turned to Jace and looked at the verse embedded in the patchwork of stained glass: You Shall Know the Truth, and the Truth Shall Set You Free.

Twenty-one

The following Saturday Amanda approached Sycamore Hill on horseback. Jace had left with Dory and Alec for Montana, and the grounds appeared deserted as she'd hoped they'd be. The first frost had arrived the night before, and although the sun was bright, a chill still lay on the hills. Amanda had finished the week in Wilmington and had come back only to ride. She glimpsed the Lydon horses in their pasture, then suddenly, drew the reins in as she caught sight of smoke curling from the carriage-house chimney. It made her heart race.

She hadn't seen David since the reception following the memorial service. He'd been a vague presence at the edge of the crowded room in the parish hall, standing with Alec while the throngs paid their respects to the Lydons. He had spoken with his ex-in-laws at length. "Renewed acquaintances" was how Amanda's father had put it. Lisa had commented on how good he looked. That evening, however, when Amanda took dinner to the Lydons, Dory had mentioned that David had left on business. It was, after all, the middle of a workweek. Without a word? Amanda, too, had returned to her office and her own house.

Now, after staring at the smoke, she nudged the horse forward. She had no idea what she would say if she found him home, no idea for that matter what was compelling her to find him. Perspiration dampened her palms, and anxiety tightened her diaphragm.

She caught sight of him as she came along the turn in the path. He was dressed for the weather in old khakis and a knit sweater. He set down a hatchet and filled his arms with split logs, straining as he turned and went into the house. There was an uncarved pumpkin on the stoop. As she rode up, he appeared in the open doorway and wiped his brow with his forearm. He sighed heavily and watched her. She stayed on the horse.

He seemed to be holding his breath as he looked up at her. "Beautiful day for a ride."

"I thought you were still away. You didn't tell me you were leaving."

"Didn't occur to me that you'd care."

"It's been a long, grueling week. I care. I appreciate all your caring—and concern."

"It was good to get away."

"Business?"

"Of sorts. Old business, same damn old business." He looked up at her and shielded his eyes. "Maybe now's the time to have you get down off that horse and come in."

The tone in his voice surprised her, and deepened the awkward silence. It was as if this were the first encounter all over again.

"David?"

"There's coffee on, and heaven knows I need the diversion." With that he disappeared through the doorway.

With her heart hammering Amanda tethered the horse and followed. She concentrated first on the changes in the familiar interior. The charming thick-walled cottage was decidedly masculine, stripped of Dory's flounces and chintz.

A fire blazed, filling the room with a faint, pleasant aroma. David came from the kitchen with two mugs. He was looking at her with a frank wariness that deepened her anxiety. She took a mug and turned to a framed watercolor over the couch. "That's a lovely painting. Wasn't it Jace's wedding present?"

"One and the same. You hated it."

"Did I? I was too young to appreciate it."

"Were you?"

"Too young." The air between them crackled as intensely as the fire. He stood between her and the window and the sunlight put a halo around his hair. "David, I feel badly that you went to Maggie's service by yourself. I didn't think. I assumed you'd sit with the Lydons. I was so caught up in my own misery—I'm sorry."

He shrugged. "Sitting in that pew stirred up a lot of memories."

She watched him over her mug. "The baptism that spring, our first Christmas Eve?"

"If we'd done things properly, I suppose we would have been married there, too."

"Yes." Her voice was a whisper. "Is it going to be like this for the rest of our lives?"

"Memories? What else is there? This is what you wanted, what you demanded of me, an empty, clean-slated future. As far as I can tell, clean slates aren't good for anything but writing down all the regrets. You wanted these empty days and nights."

"Not to relive every stupid argument and thought-less moment we ever shared."

He put down his mug. "Is that what you've been doing?"

"Yes, more and more." She looked at his dark eyes. "I'm scared to death, David."

"I hope it's a healthy fear, the kind that makes your nerves dance."

Adrenaline rushed through her veins, slapping her with reality. "Are you seeing anyone else?"

Amazement shifted his features. "Is that what you're afraid of?"

"Yes." There. She'd said it. "Suddenly."

"Is there any reason why I shouldn't?"

"No, I suppose not." She listened to the thunder in her chest and the voice in her heart, then the sound of one deep sigh. "Yes. Yes, there is."

David rocked back on his heels. "What might that be?"

"You're making this very difficult," she whispered.

"God, I hope so. I've about had it with this no-man's-land we're living in. This isn't a life, Amanda, not for me, anyway."

David stood still as he spoke, empowered by her re-action. Hope filled a thousand empty spaces in him, still tempered, however, by the doubt in her voice. It would have been so easy to reassure her, to pull Amanda into his arms and tell her there was no one else, that no one else had ever come close to giving him what he'd found so briefly with her. He swallowed the words and the desire.

"I need time to work this through," she said.

"To work what through?"

Her eyes flashed; her reticence seemed to melt. "You know exactly what."

"Say it."

"This half-baked notion that there might still be something between us."

"Something."

"Yes, something."

"Give it a name, Amanda."

"Not until I can recognize it."

David turned from her to the hills laid out beyond the window. Leaves swirled on his patch of lawn. He seemed to be growing buoyant, spirited at her insinuation. He smiled at the view but kept his tone low. "When might your vision clear? I don't intend to go through this adolescent misery another time."

"How can you tease?"

"There's been little enough humor in my life lately."

"I might still be in love with you, David."

"That's the something between us?"

"Maybe." She paused. "What if I fail you again?"

"No reason why you should."

"Commitment . . ."

"Would do us both a world of good."

"We should never have become lovers again."

"We should never have stopped in the first place."

"Love takes commitment. It's so much safer to stay away from you."

He touched her cheek. "You and I weren't made for anything safe."

"I know that. I've tried. You know how hard—to stay away. I can't seem to make myself."

He smiled slowly and stepped to her, as close as a heartbeat. "Maybe there is justice after all."

He pulled her into an embrace. While his arms were around her, he leaned her back and kissed her until she was warm and pliant between his arms and his unyielding body. Her mouth was slightly open in surprise. He felt the heat of soft, familiar places. The moment he broke from the kiss she gasped for air, simply deepening his desire.

David touched her hair. "Maggie's death was a terrible loss, but it's given you back to me. Since the night she was hospitalized, you haven't had the strength for pretense. For once you were forced to lean on me. For once I was able to reach out and find nothing but you. And whether you realize it or not you took everything I offered, every ounce of support. You're right that I left without a word. It was just a matter of time until you recovered your perfect equilibrium. Frankly I didn't have the stamina to stay here while you pushed me aside, brushed yourself off and got on with your life. *Again.*"

"I haven't."

"Not this time? That Sunday when you saw our picture in the paper was my first glimpse of another you. No pretense, just vulnerability." He smiled at her. "Raw, desperate need is an intriguing trait to find in a woman of your strength."

"I'd like you to stick around, David."

"Why?"

She paused. "Because it's getting impossible to brush myself off. I can't push you aside any longer. I don't want to," she whispered.

He had intended for the banter to stay light. He had been so sure he'd finally gotten the upper hand. He looked out at the dying sunlight in the bordering woods. "Out here there's a balance. In this place I can feel an incredible sense of rightness, of purpose. Come here, Dazzle." With his nerves in turmoil he opened his arms to her. He was wound as tightly as a wire. Anticipation made him ache.

"I know you'll let me touch you. We were meant for this. We let too much get in the way." He slowly moved his hand along the side of her throat. "You can call it anything—fate, faith, pure coincidence. We're back in each other's lives, for better, not worse. I made a vow. I gave you my word. I promised to love and cherish you in good times and rotten times."

"There were rotten times," she whispered.

"And there may be again. That's not enough reason to quit." He moved his hand to her ribs and his voice grew husky. "Do you know, I sit at my drawing board sometimes and stare at my hand. I think about the soft weight of your breasts and the curve of your hips and I can't work. What we have together isn't idle curiosity. The bond's still there. We've been given a second chance."

"The bond was broken."

He crushed her to him. "Then mend it with me. Give me the chance to take pride in what you do. Be proud of me again. Tell me. I need it. You make me whole. We've been lovers. We're getting to be friends."

"Most men—"

"Amanda, darling, I'm not most men. I am, I hope, a more mature version of the only man you promised to love, honor and cherish."

"Thank goodness we had obey written out of the ceremony."

"Obey your heart, obey your soul and it comes around to the same thing."

"I love you," she gasped as he undid her jacket.

"I know, Dazzle. That's been the hell of it, watching you try to bury it or ignore it." She tried to kiss him, but he held her at arm's length. "Talk to me, darling. Talk and listen to your own words." He pulled his sweater over his head.

"It's not easy. I love you, I need you, David. I need you to understand what I don't understand myself. I don't want to hurt you, and I can't bear to be hurt again. I thought not seeing you, refusing to think about it, would make it go away. It only made the separation worse."

The overwound spring in David's chest began to loosen. Hope heated his words. "This time was agony."

"If you'll believe me, I want a chance to make things right, starting now. Make love to me, David."

"Marry me. Make Marco happy. Prove what Maggie suspected all along. You won't be sorry," he managed as he crushed her against him.

They suspended conversation, apologies and proposals as they fell into each other's arms in front of the fire. Perfect rhythm came immediately and confirmed what they both knew.

"It was never as right as this," he gasped as they shimmered in the heat and the pleasure and the relief of a decision mutually made at last.

Long moments later, bathed in the light from the open window, Amanda stroked his chest. "There's a quotation under the stained-glass window that I kept reading at Mrs. Lydon's service, reading it as if I were seeing it for the first time." She turned and kissed him. "Is it sacrilege to apply it to us?"

"You shall know the truth," he murmured.

"I love you."

"And the truth shall set you free."

* * * * *

SILHOUETTE® *Desire*™ MAN OF THE MONTH

YOU'VE ASKED FOR IT, YOU'VE GOT IT!
MAN OF THE MONTH: 1992

ONLY FROM SILHOUETTE DESIRE

You just couldn't get enough of them, those men from Silhouette Desire—twelve sinfully sexy, delightfully devilish heroes. Some will make you sweat, some will make you sigh . . . but every long, lean one of them will have you swooning. So here they are, *more* of the men we couldn't resist bringing to you for one more year. . . .

BEST MAN FOR THE JOB
by Dixie Browning in June

MIDNIGHT RIDER
by Cait London in July

CONVENIENT HUSBAND
by Joan Hohl in August

NAVARRONE
by Helen R. Myers in September

A MAN OF HONOR
by Paula Detmer Riggs in October

BLUE SKY GUY
by Carole Buck in November

IT HAD TO BE YOU
by Jennifer Greene in December

Don't let these men get away! MAN OF THE MONTH, only in Silhouette Desire!

MOM92JD

Silhouette CHRISTMAS Stories 1992

Experience the beauty of Yuletide romance with Silhouette Christmas Stories 1992—a collection of heartwarming stories by favorite Silhouette authors.

JONI'S MAGIC by Mary Lynn Baxter
HEARTS OF HOPE by Sondra Stanford
THE NIGHT SANTA CLAUS RETURNED by Marie Ferrarella
BASKET OF LOVE by Jeanne Stephens

Also available this year are three popular early editions of Silhouette Christmas Stories—1986, 1987 and 1988. Look for these and you'll be well on your way to a complete collection of the best in holiday romance.

Plus, as an added bonus, you can receive a FREE keepsake Christmas ornament. Just collect four proofs of purchase from any November or December 1992 Harlequin or Silhouette series novels, or from any Harlequin or Silhouette Christmas collection, and receive a beautiful dated brass Christmas candle ornament.

Mail this certificate along with four (4) proof-of-purchase coupons, plus $1.50 postage and handling (check or money order—do not send cash), payable to Silhouette Books, to: **In the U.S.**: P.O. Box 9057, Buffalo, NY 14269-9057; **In Canada**: P.O. Box 622, Fort Erie, Ontario, L2A 5X3.

ONE PROOF OF PURCHASE	Name: _____
	_____
	Address: _____
	_____
	City: _____
	State/Province: _____
SX92POP	Zip/Postal Code: _____

093 KAG